SEARCH FOR BLUE WOLF

BY

TARRIE A. MCBRIDE

BASED ON TARRIE A. MCBRIDE'S
SCREENPLAY - COWBOYS AND DINOSAURS

Inquiries and Book Orders should be addressed to:

Great Writers Media
Email: info@greatwritersmedia.com
Phone: 877-600-5469

ISBN: 979-8-89175-108-8 (sc)
ISBN: 979-8-89175-109-5 (ebk)

EXT HUMID JUNGLE SETTING -100 MILLION YEARS AGO-DAY

A lone surviving twelve year old boy, TIMOTHY MACROY, sits against a prehistoric fern tree. It's the meeting place. An arrow shot high above the trunk marked the place to enter and exit. It is the passageway through time; worlds of dynamically different species. Young Tim waits.

                        PTERADACTYL
                EEEE! RAAAA!EEEE! RAAAA!

A huge Pteradactyl flies overhead belching a loud screech. The forty foot flying creature's shadow travels the lush floor. It doesn't see the boy or it would snatch him for food. Roars from "T" Rex are heard in the distance.

                          T REX
                RRRRRROOAARRRRRRR!!!!!

Hundreds of smaller Bat-like flying dinosaurs are startled by it and fly from the trees. The leaves rattle. Strange noises fill the air. Dark clouds move in; the thunder claps and rain drenches the jungle landscape.

                    TIMOTHY MACROY (VO)
              I never thought it would come to this? I'm trapped
                without the others. It's tough now without Dad and
              Virginia. I think about how grand it was when we started
                this adventure. What twelve year old kid wouldn't?

EXT. DAKOTA SIOUX INDIAN CAMP NEAR BLACK HILLS-SOUTH DAKOTA - NIGHT (FROM DISTANCE)

A dark moonless sky covers the rugged terrain.
Stars sparkle so bright they hurt your eyes. Rolling waves of campfire light reflect on the tepees. The drums beat and the braves chant. The year is 1880.

EXT. INDIAN CAMP NEAR BLACK HILLS-SOUTH DAKOTA
-NIGHT (ZOOM IN TO FIRESIDE)

The council fire crackles and the embers spit. Dakota Sioux gather around it. Sioux Eagle dancers spread wings and weave a story with their rhythmic footwork. Chief Red Eagle smokes the peace pipe and the wavering light reveals the faces. The great White Hunters who are friends with the Sioux are also here. John MacRoy and his companions, have heard strange stories from traders who know these native hunters.

> CHIEF RED EAGLE
> (In the Dakota language) Five moons ago,"Painted Horse" and "BLUE WOLF" left camp with other braves to hunt buffalo. That is when it happened.

> JOHN MACROY
> (to the interpreter in Scottish accent)
> Everette, ask him what happened?

> EVERETTE KIRBY
> (In Dakota)
> Chief what happened?

> CHIEF RED EAGLE
> I will let Painted Horse tell you.

Painted Horse walks to the Chief to speak.

FLASHBACK

EXT PLAINS NEAR THE BLACK HILL -DAY

Everette interprets, and illustrates a picture of the hunt. We're taken back to the charging beast in several brief, but graphic, pictures that fly at you faster than you can comprehend.

PAINTED HORSE
The buffalo were down below us. I waited for "Straight Arrow"
to give us the signal. BLUE WOLF was starting down, when out
of the air the white beast from the Spirit World came. It speared
my horse upon its three horns and shook me to the ground.

CHIEF RED EAGLE
Tell them what happened to BLUE WOLF.

A quick vision of, Painted Horse, being attacked.

PAINTED HORSE
The white beast turned to attack me on the ground, when
BLUE WOLF shot several arrows into it. The white devil
beast was mad and chased BLUE WOLF. They ripped
(MORE) PAINTED HORSE (cont'd) through the air. He
and his horse vanished, chased by this evil creature, back
to the devil world. The air opened to swallow them.
They vanished.

Eyes are wide open in the circle as the story unfolds. John MacRoy
speaks to Everette.

JOHN MACROY
It's bloody unbelievable!! Just
like the fur trappers said in the bar.

FLASHBACK

INT. WHISKEY CREEK BAR, WHISKEY CREEK SOUTH
DAKOTA- DAY

A rough & tumble wild-west bar, piano keys plinking out a tune
of "She'll Be Comin' Round The Mountain" and "Down By The
Old Mill Stream". A poker game was going, the professional girls
were sizing up their "customers" and pushing drinks for the bar. John

MacRoy was at the bar with two scraggly looking trappers, dressed in leather and furs. They are intoxicated to say the least.

TRAPPER #1
Ya see-eee, Mr. Mac....what did you
say your name was agaaaaain?

JOHN MACROY
MacRoy, John MacRoy.

TRAPPER #1
Right, MacRoy, as I was fixin' to say, I have information from
the Sioux injuns around River Fork, ya' know Chief Red Eagle's
camp,that some braves huntin' buffalo ran into some giant creature
that attacked two buffalo scouts and almost killed the one.

TRAPPER #2
....Then vanished in thin air!

TRAPPER #1
Aw come on Lukey, It was my turn to tell the story.

JOHN MACROY
It's OK. Now tell me, how many people know about this?

TRAPPER #1
Just us trappers and them injuns. And oh
yeah, now you too, MacRoy.

JOHN MACROY
So tell me gents, and I use that term loosely, did the
Indians tell you what this creature looked like?

TRAPPER #2
They said he looked like a giant lizard with
horns like a buffalo, but way bigger!

TRAPPER #1
Now Luke, I was supposed to tell it!

JOHN MACROY
SHHHHHHHH! Keep it down boys. I don't
want the whole world to know.

The bartender slides down the bar approaching John's left ear as the
trappers are distracted by the girls and the music.

BARTENDER
John, maybe not the whole world, but the whole bar's
heard the story except for a few whores upstairs.

The bartender pauses to think.

BARTENDER
(cont)On second thought, these trappers have been
fairly loud. The girls upstairs know as well.

JOHN MACROY
Oh. OK boys, it's about time for us to leave.

TRAPPER #1
Not so fast. I think we deserve a little
somethin' for that information.

JOHN MACROY
Now what did you boys have in mind?

TRAPPER #1
How about, buyin' us... a bottle of whiskey?

JOHN MACROY
Bartender, could you give these two mountain
gentleman a bottle of your best...on me of course.

                         BARTENDER
            You bet John, it's the best cause it's all I got.

                         TRAPPER #2
                And that's good enough for me.

                         TRAPPER #1
                      and me toooo!

RETURN TO:

EXT. INDIAN CAMP NEAR BLACK HILLS-SOUTH DAKOTA
-NIGHT (ZOOM IN TO FIRESIDE)

                        JOHN MACROY
        Ya know Everette,just think, one minute we're in the
            bar talking about this. The next minute we're here
                livin' the dream. We're gonna find those....

John sees an opening for them to talk to the Chief.

                        JOHN MACROY
        Everette, ask him if we can speak with Painted Horse.

                       EVERETTE KIRBY
        Chief, with great respect we ask your permission to speak
        to Painted Horse to see if he can add something to this.

The Chief talks with his second in command and he escorts Painted
Horse to sit next to MacRoy and Everette.

CHIEF RED EAGLE
Answer any questions the great white
hunter, McRoy, might ask you.

MacRoy is offered the peace pipe by a Sioux, takes a quick drag and passes it on.

JOHN MACROY
(gasping)
I need to know exactly what this creature looked like. Can you have him tell me? Better yet Everette, have the savage draw me a picture.

EVERETTE KIRBY
Painted Horse, could you draw a picture with this stick
in the dirt. What did this "White Beast" look like?

He hands him a stick and he draws something that looked like a rhinoceros with a giant collar. MacRoy draws his drawing on paper.

JOHN MACROY
Now ask him how big the brute is?

EVERETTE KIRBY
Could you tell us how big this creature was?

PAINTED HORSE
I hope you believe me. The beast was four times larger
than a bull buffalo. It stood as tall as the "iron horse"
and had three horns and a mouth like an eagle.

JOHN MACROY
Ask him if he could take us back to the spot where it happened?

EVERETTE KIRBY
Can you take us back to the place where this happened?

The Chief speaks up as many of the braves are discontent.

JOHN MACROY
Aye, Everette what in Sam hill has happened to this friendly group?
Are we in for a wee bit of trouble here?

EVERETTE KIRBY
Well boss, the Black Hills are sacred to the Sioux and other
(MORE)

EVERETTE KIRBY (cont'd)
neighboring tribes, like the Kiowa and Cheyenne. We
need another angle if we're gonna' tame them down.

JOHN MACROY
I've got it. Tell them that I was told in a dream to kill the white
spirit beast and return "BLUE WOLF" safely to his tribe. The white
magic must be broken by a white man. Go ahead Everette, tell him.

Everette looks at John with a squint and wrinkled forehead, as if to
pause before lying.

EVERETTE KIRBY
Chief, Mr. MacRoy had a dream several days ago. He was to kill
a white spirit beast and return a brave to his tribe. It will take a
white man to break the bad magic of this evil white spirit beast.

The Chief turns to whisper in the ear of his second in command.
They pause. The Chief calls out to his medicine man. He appears
with his headdress of a buffalo head and fur. He walks with a feath-
ered covered lance and has pouches tied to his buffalo leather outfit.
He shakes his head and begins to dance and chant. He throws dust
from his pouches into the air, then talks to the council. Now the
Chief speaks.

CHIEF RED EAGLE
It has been five moons since BLUE WOLF entered the
Spirit World. Our ancestors have not greeted him to the
happy hunting grounds. Our medicine man has told me
BLUE WOLF is alive, trapped by the evil spirits.
MacRoy you must set BLUE WOLF free.

The Chief whispers in the ear of his second in command, then speaks.

JOHN MACROY
Aye, now what?

Three Sioux braves come from out out the fire council and stand by the
Chief. They lower and raise their heads as the Chief calls their name.

CHIEF RED EAGLE
I will send Painted
Horse, Straight Arrow and Big Bear to guide you.
They're good warriors that can track game many miles.
Painted Horse will show you where he and BLUE WOLF
fought the creature. You will leave at sun up.

JOHN MACROY
What did he say? Are we on our bloody adventure or did he say no?

EVERETTE KIRBY
We're on John, and the Chief is giving us three warriors to
help in our quest. One of them is Painted Horse. He alone
knows where the last place the white beast was seen.

JOHN MACROY
That's grand! We must start packing now to get a start on the
'morrow. Did you remember to send that telegraph to Miss
Deven to come with her gauchos and her dinosaur professor.

EVERETTE KIRBY
That I did sir, and they are meetin' us at
the Cheyenne River crossing.

JOHN MACROY
Good, good..it's coming together.

The Chief makes an announcement

CHIEF RED EAGLE
Now all braves must dance around the fire and call our
ancestors to guide and watch over you on your journey.

JOHN MACROY
Aye, we can't stay any longer, what did the Chief say?

EVERETTE KIRBY
Well, trappers who have insulted the Chief by not
staying for his spirit dancer send off, have been
(MORE)

EVERETTE KIRBY (cont'd)
buried by the Cheyenne River, what was left of them.

JOHN MACROY
Oh I love a good send off, that I do!

EVERETTE KIRBY
It's mighty good in my book as well.

They settle in to enjoy the celebration, as they smile and bob their
heads at the Chief in appreciation. The Chief walks over to John
during the dance.

CHIEF RED EAGLE
I'm told you have a son, great white hunter. "BLUE
WOLF' is my only son. If you are successful and return
him to me, I will give you all of the Black Hills land that
the Great White Father in Washington gave to us.

EVERETTE KIRBY)
Jumpin Jehossaphat! John this deal is getting interestin'.

JOHN MAC ROY
What's he bloody sayin'?

Everette motions him to wait.

CHIEF RED EAGLE
You can have the gold and we will live in the land at peace with
you. Your son will also be my son and BLUE WOLF will also
be yours. This will make the dream world come to pass. We will
celebrate upon your mighty return. If you fail to find BLUE
WOLF, this will be an omen that our tribe of Dakota Sioux will
join the Cheyenne and the Kiowa to fight against the white man.

EVERETTE KIRBY
John, "Red Eagle"'s offerin us the Black Hills and all the gold
in it if we return his son, BLue Wolf. It has only one catch.

JOHN MAC ROY
So don't keep me in suspenders Laddie, what's the catch?

EVERETTE KIRBY
Well...If we fail to return with him, he's at
war with us and all other Whites.

JOHN MAC ROY
Oh. (pause) Well that put's a twist in the Old Man's kilts. A
pure like it!(I really like it!) We're on our bloody hunt!

TIMOTHY MACROY (VO)
Dad told me about the bloomin' council meetin'. I thought
it great to hear his plans come together, but I didn't hear
about the son swapping stuff 'till later. I was hopin' they didn't
mean a permanent exchange. I just shut up and rode.

EXT PLAINS NEAR THE BLACK HILLS - CONTINUOUS
-DAY BREAK

They pull out from the Sioux Camp. The three braves join the hunting trip. There are six men on horse back along side a wagon drawn
by a team of Clydesdales.

JOHN MACROY
Come on mates! Let's get a move on it! Times a wastin'.

The two men that drive the wagon are "FRENCHY" Francois La
Rue and "BIG BEN" Carver, Frenchy is a renowned kick
boxer in France that came to America for fame and fortune. He also
carries a large Bowie knife and knows how to use it. Big Ben is a son
of a freed slave that came West with the money he won bare knuckle
fighting in Alabama. "TEX LAWSON" is on horseback. He is a trick
roper and rodeo rider.

JOHN MACROY
(cont)
Ben! You must be able to see all of the
Dakotas from your perch up there?!

BIG BEN
I surely do Master John.

JOHN MACROY
You're a free man, Ben. I'm not your master, but
I am a Mister. Call me Mister John.

BIG BEN
I hear ya' Mister John.

Ben has a tender spirit and loves kids. He's young Timothy MacRoy's
protector. The horse drawn wagon is to rendezvous with the rest of
the hunting party.

JOHN MACROY
Don't ye forget, we're meetin' up with the others
near the Cheyenne River crossing.

FRENCHY
Oui, Monsieur MacRoy. The place is in my head. I will not forget.

BIG BEN
No worries Mister MacRoy, Big Ben is keepin' a close eye
on everything, too. Including young Timothy MacRoy.

Timothy MacRoy, John MacRoy's twelve year old son, pops his head
out from the wagon to talk to his Dad.

TIMOTHY MACROY
Aye dad, how come I couldn't attend the big Pow Wow last
night? I had lots of questions to ask. I could have...

JOHN MACROY
Look son, I heard that if the Sioux had known you were there, we
all would be forced to eat you over the council fire for breakin'
the bloody Sioux rules against youths attendin' the Fire Council.

He winks at Everette.

TIMOTHY MACROY
Not so! I've never read anything of the like, and I'm well
read on the Dakota, Oglala and Hunkpapa Sioux.

Everette rides up close to the wagon.

JOHN MACROY
Everette, tell this boy that had he gone to the
council meetin' last night we would have had to
roast him over that very fire and eat him.

EVERETTE KIRBY
Oh that's a fact, cross my heart. Them injuns don't take
kindly to youngin's sneakin' into their meetings. You'd
be a hush puppy with stew on every brave's plate.

TIMOTHY MACROY
Aw Kirby, you're so full of it. Look, your nose is growin'.

He checks the end of his nose with his index finger.

EVERETTE KIRBY
No it ain't?

TIMOTHY MACROY
Ha, ha, ha. Made ya' look.

EVERETTE KIRBY
Why you little...

TEX LAWSON
Looks like the youngin' took it back at ya', Everette.

Timothy pops back in the confines of the inner wagon just as an
arrow sticks in the wagon close to Frenchy. Ben inspects the arrow.

BIG BEN
It's Pawnee! They hates da Sioux and cowpoke too. Take cover!
Pawnee!

Two, three and four arrows stick in the wagon. The wagon stops and the horsemen fall back. The Sioux braves motion to John MacRoy to wait as they go out to find their enemy.

JOHN MACROY
Hold your fire! Hold your fire! The Sioux
scouts are goin' out to give

JOHN MACROY (cont'd)
a look-see. Don't shoot the wrong Indian.
Ya hear?! Put your guns down!

They sneak up on foot. Painted Horse draws his bow and shoots one. A Pawnee yipes a war cry and attacks him with a knife. Big Bear Grabs him from behind and chokes him lifeless.

PAINTED HORSE
Ona hanee. (In the trees)

They see four more Pawnee in the trees. Straight arrow motions to the others for position. They all draw their bows and send arrows flying. The dead enemy braves drop from their perch. They spread out again to see if any others. There's no sign of danger. They return to the wagon. Everette questions them in the Dakota tongue.

EVERETTE KIRBY
Did you see any Pawnee?

PAINTED HORSE
Yes...They are all dead Pawnee.

He holds six scalps up on his stringer.

JOHN MACROY
OK men, Let's get a move on it. It looks like our
Sioux friends have stopped the attack. It's OK.

TIMOTHY MACROY
They missed me.

EVERETTE KIRBY
It was too close for comfort, boy.

They start up the trek again. Where they're headed is still a mystery.

TIMOTHY MACROY (VO)
Little did I know that this was nothing compared to what
lay ahead. It was a small piece to a difficult puzzle.

JOHN MACROY

Everette, that's my boy. Like it or not, I had to pull him out of the
university. The lad is the smartest of the bunch at school. I just

JOHN MACROY (cont'd)
couldn't bare to see him miss out on all the adventure
since the lad's mother died a year ago.

EVERETTE KIRBY
Sorry to hear that sir.

JOHN MACROY
It's a chance for some man to man stuff. Father and son.

EVERETTE KIRBY
I hear ya' Mac. It's good.

Everette pulls his horse back behind the wagon.

BIG BEN
Mister MacRoy, how much longer before
we meet up with the others?

JOHN MACROY
We have about two more hours, then we'll stop for coffee
and breakfast when we meet up on the Cheyenne. (river)

BIG BEN
That be good, 'cause Big Ben's hungry enough to eat
one of these team horses all by hisself...tail first.

JOHN MACROY
Ha, ha, I bet you could Ben, ha, ha, but then
you would have to pull the wagon.

BIG BEN
See, looky here, there's always a catch in a man's good plans.

JOHN MACROY
You're right Ben. Let's keep them horses
movin' along. It won't be long.

BIG BEN
They be movin' like a steam engine train mister Mac.

He cracks the whip.

BIG BEN
(cont')
Giddy up you big 'uns. Brother Ben's gonna' have
some good hay for you when we stop.

TWO HOURS LATER

TIMOTHY MACROY (VO)
Yes, we made it. I remember how good it was to see
the others. Little did I know what was in store.

EXT CHEYENNE RIVER RENDEZVOUS SITE -DAY

They follow the river toward the meeting place.

FRENCHY
Look! They're over there. I see the others.

A joyous spirit draws them all the faster. Ben drives the horses.

BIG BEN
Move it on. Snap!(whip) We gonna be there
directly horses. Snap! Uncle Ben is hung-ry!

The Chinese cook, Kan Wu, called "COOKIE", pops his head out of the wagon to see for the first time.

COOKIE
It time for chow. Chow time.

John MacRoy's company meets up with VIRGINIA DEVEN'S Company. Sweetheart to John MacRoy and Wild West trick shot artist, she demands respect from all men. Young Timothy MacRoy doesn't know about her since his mom's death.

JOHN MACROY
Let's get these wagons together over here,
and Cookie, get the vittles goin'!

COOKIE
Cookie get chow chop, chop. Fast, fast.

Virginia Devens sees John and runs over to him. They embrace and kiss casually in mixed company. Young Tim sees and doesn't understand. His dad calls to him.

TIMOTHY MACROY (VO)
The first time I saw her I was furious. I
wanted not to like her, but couldn't.

JOHN MACROY
Timothy, please come here I would like to introduce
you to a good friend of mine, Miss Virginia Deven.

TIMOTHY MACROY
Hello... Dad, have you forgotten about Mom already?

Tim turns and rudely walks away.

JOHN MACROY
Son, you get back here right now or...

Virginia Interjects.

VIRGINIA DEVEN
John, the boy needs time. We just met.
Give it time. Let me talk to him.

She walks over to Tim as he arrives at the wagon.

VIRGINIA DEVEN
Hi Tim, I appreciate what you said back there.
My mom died when I was eight and dad took
on a young bride shortly thereafter.

TIMOTHY MACROY
He did?

VIRGINIA DEVEN
She was a small chicken in a big hen house. My brother and I
didn't like her at first. Until she taught us some things. Hey, would
ya' like to help me after chow to practice shooting my rifles?

TIMOTHY MACROY
Sure, I guess.

VIRGINIA DEVEN
Ok, meet me here after vittles. Deal?

TIMOTHY MACROY
Deal.

Virginia walks over to the chow line and mingles with the boys.

COOKIE
Ok! I cook eggs, bacon, beans and rice. You have coffee ova'
dere. I have goats milk and biscuits ova' here. You like?!

BIG BEN
The line starts behind me, and I sho' hope you gents
have somethin' left to eat when I get through.

FRENCHY
Ben if there is no food, we may be forced to eat
YOU in place of the bacon. Ha. Ha.

BIG BEN
With all the fightin' I been doin' I'd be a pretty tough meat.

COOKIE
You no worry, Cookie can cook you. Chinese are best cooks.

Everyone laughs.

JOHN MACROY
Now listen up! You have about 2 hours rest. Eat, then
water and feed the horses. We have a meeting to discuss
the expedition I have hired you for. Now rest up.

Virginia walks over to John.

VIRGINIA DEVEN
Let's sit over here so we can talk.

JOHN MACROY
Alright then. I can't resist a beautiful woman.

VIRGINIA DEVEN
John, save it for a minute. I talked with Timothy and he is a good
boy. I like him. Let it run it's course. Some things take time.

JOHN MACROY
But, I thought...

VIRGINIA DEVEN
You don't have to think. That's the beauty of it. I'll take it from
here. We're shooting my rifles after vittles. It's a good thing John.

JOHN MACROY
Now I know why I love this woman.

He bends down and they kiss.

TIMOTHY MACROY (VO)
It was easy to like Virginia. In a way I liked her to the point of
being jealous of Dad. She turned out to be a good friend.

ONE HOUR IS PASSED AND EVERYONE'S FINISHED EATING

Virginia walks over to Tim.

VIRGINIA DEVEN
Hi, Tim. Are you ready to learn some shooting?

TIMOTHY MACROY
Yep, sure.

They walk out to an open field near the river

                    VIRGINIA DEVEN
              Ok, do you like candy wafers?

                    TIMOTHY MACROY
                         A little.

                    VIRGINIA DEVEN
      Here take these wafers and throw them as high as you
        can over there toward the river. Tell me when?

She waits casually with her rifle.

                    TIMOTHY MACROY
                           Ok

                    VIRGINIA DEVEN
        Alright throw them in the air one at a time
              and really high over the river.

He throws, BANG! it explodes. He throws, BANG! it explodes. He
throws, BANG it explodes

                    VIRGINIA DEVEN
                         (cont)
          Now throw a handful of five wafers.

He throws, Bang! Bang! Bang! Bang! Bang! all wafers are hit. The
whole camp applauds.

                    TIMOTHY MACROY
                  That's great Virginia!

Onlookers clap and hoot.

VIRGINIA DEVEN
OK, now it's your turn.

TIMOTHY MACROY
I don't know?

VIRGINIA DEVEN
Here hold the rifle like this. When the wafer is
thrown into the air you feel the position with a
quick fire turn and shoot. Now try it. Here.

She throws the wafer up. BANG and a miss.

VIRGINIA DEVEN
Let's try it again, Ready, here goes.

She throws the wafer up. BANG and a miss.

VIRGINIA DEVEN
Now I want you to pretend that you're drawing a dot
on the wafer with a pencil, but the pencil is your rifle.
Pull the trigger when you want to draw. Ready?

She throws the wafer into the air. BANG! It's a hit

TIMOTHY MACROY
Alright!

VIRGINIA DEVEN
Again...Ready?

She throws the wafer in the air BANG! it's a hit.

TIMOTHY MACROY
That is so fun. Thank you Miss Deven.

VIRGINIA DEVEN
Oh, you're so very welcome.

TIMOTHY MACROY
By the way, you said you didn't like your dad's bride
until she taught you some things. What things?

VIRGINIA DEVEN
Oh. How to shoot rifles and pistols. Her name
was later known as Annie Oakley.

Back at Chow two men are fist fighting. It's Big Ben and one of Miss
Deven's cowhands, an Argentinian Gaucho named Juan Bartelli.

FRENCHY
Sacre Bleu! Ben, get him.

Juan throws three quick jabs in Ben's face. Ben counters with an
upper cut that lifts Juan off the ground. Back on their feet they continue to exchange blows. Virginia goes to John.

TEX LAWSON
Come on Ben!

JOSE LAGANA
Ultra base, Juan, mas duro! (Again Juan, Harder)

VIRGINIA DEVEN
What's this all about John?

JOHN MACROY
Aye Missy, the boys here got to braggin' whose group had
the stronger fist man. We believe it to be Big Ben.

CROWD
Get 'em Ben! No, Juan in the stomach! Look out!

She pulls out her six shooter and shoots a button off of Ben's suspender BLAM! and it falls, then a loop off of Juans' belt line. BLAM! They stop...and look to the direction of fire.

VIRGINIA DEVEN
Now we are here to work together. Save your talents
for what's ahead...you may need them.

JOHN MACROY
Sweetheart, it was all in good fun.

VIRGINIA DEVEN
John, have you ever seen a seasoned gaucho use his bola?

JOHN MACROY
Don't be talkin' dirty to me. Ha, Ha. No I
can't recall ever witnessing such.

VIRGINIA DEVEN
Juan is the best of his breed. He can take an animal down
with his bolas in seconds. I don't want that talent hurt
in a stupid bare knuckle contest. You understand my
love?! And I know you and young Tim like Ben.

JOHN MACROY
I'm beginnin' to get the picture. Alright, it's time for our meeting
before we go further. COME ON OVER HERE...EVERYONE!

TIMOTHY MACROY (VO)
Dad was good at getting to the point. He just reminded
us why we all were here. Some would definitely forget.

The fighters lick their wounds and walk over with the rest.

They all circle around John. The three Dakota Sioux braves gather to the outside of the circle.

JOHN MACROY (CONT.)
I've been a hunter ever since I could remember from a young
lad shootin' pheasant to huntin' grizzlies, elk and moose here
in the States. The bigger and meaner the better I say.

The crowd chimes in.

CROWD
Yeah we hear ya'. That's a fact Mr. MacRoy.

JOHN MACROY
I want to introduce a man I called to be here based on that bigger
and meaner statement. His name is Mister Perkins and he is a
Professor of Paleontology. He studies DINOSAURS and the like.

EVERETTE KIRBY
Boss, I'm sorry. He doesn't look like anything
bigger and meaner to me.

JOHN MACROY
The dinosaurs are the bigger and meaner ones.

PROFESSOR PERKINS
Ah...yes...If I may. I was brought to this expedition quite by
chance. I study the bones of creatures that lived over 100
million years ago Timothy MacRoy is a student in my class.

FRENCHY
So why do we care if old bones existed?

PROFESSOR PERKINS
A good question. It was described to me that recently, a
fantastic creature appeared out of nowhere and attacked
a Sioux buffalo hunter. From the accounts I received...
the creature appears to be this prehistoric animal.

He pulls a black lined drawing from his carrying satchel.

PROFESSOR PERKINS
(cont)
This is triceratops. A huge herbivor...

EVERETTE KIRBY
In English?

PROFESSOR PERKINS
Oh sorry...A large grass eating dinosaur with three huge horns.

The three Sioux braves move closer to see.

PAINTED HORSE
(in Dakota)
Look! It is the White beast from hell! It's him.
That is the evil one.

PROFESSOR PERKINS
I have heard of this intriguing encounter...but this creature
appears to be docile from our studies? And how could
it appear 100 million years later? It may be an albino,
which would account for it's frustrated behavior.

JOHN MACROY
Excuse me and I'll say it to the all of ya'. That's what I'm
payin' ya for. We are goin' to find that entrance to this place
where these creature came from and I'm fixin' to take a trophy.
Ben would you bring one of my special rifles over here.

Ben pulls a heavy wooden crate over to John.

BIG BEN
Here be yo' guns Mister MacRoy.

He takes a crowbar and pries the lid from this coffin-like crate and hands one to John. It has the appearance of a large dinosaur gun with a rotary magazine like a "Tommy Gun".

JOHN MACROY

I had this gun designed by my good friend Mr. Gatling.
I just want to give this creature a sportin' chance.

He looks over to his sweetheart and says.

JOHN MACROY
(cont)

My love, can you prop up this metal sign of a bear
against that cotton wood tree over there.

Young Tim takes it.

TIMOTHY MACROY

Let me do it Miss Deven.

VIRGINIA DEVEN

Sure.

Tim runs it out to the tree next to the river.

TIMOTHY MACROY

Where do you want it? Here dad?

JOHN MACROY

A little to the left leaning against the tree...Right there, son.

TIMOTHY MACROY

Got it!

JOHN MACROY
Now come away from there lad. More than a wee
bit. Even back to the wagons would be good.

He runs to the wagons.

JOHN MACROY
(cont)
If that bear were our tri cera beast,

He commences firing and it cuts the bear in half, machine gun style
and proceeds to fall the tree. The rounds continue to travel, clearing
weeds and splashing in the river!

The crowd is first silent. Then one cowpoke yelps with the crowd.

CROWD
Yaa-hoo! We're goin' on a Dinosaur hunt! Yeah! Alright!

TEX LAWSON
And I'm fixin to rope me one as sure as my name's TEX.

TIMOTHY MACROY (VO)
We sure had our adrenaline moving. We didn't know where we
were headed, but we were goin' there, and we were going to shoot
a dinosaur. That's what some of us were thinking at any rate.

EXT CHEYENNE RIVER CROSSING -DAY -CONTINUOUS

The expedition crosses over the river toward upper plains of the Black
Hills. The Sioux braves lead the way. The wagons bring up the rear.
Miss Deven and John ride horseback beside one another.

VIRGINIA DEVEN
John, did you ever think we'd be doing something
like this six months before we marry?

JOHN MACROY
No my love. I'd say if we top this on our honeymoon,
our marriage has a good chance of makin' it.

VIRGINIA DEVEN
I love to rise to the occasion my love...we'll definitely top it.

JOHN MACROY
That's why I love this lady. She has a plan for everything!

The party trudges up the steps of the Black Hills looking for the cosmic site, that tear in the time warp.

FOUR HOURS LATER-the wagons pull together.

EXT PLAINS NEAR THE BLACK HILLS -NIGHTFALL

BIG BEN
Whoa whoa! You horses stop so brother Ben can
care fo' you and gets you all ready fo'de night.

He pulls them behind Miss Devens wagon. "Cookie" gets out to get dinner started.

COOKIE
Me need fire if you want Cookie to make
chow. You get wood. Chop, chop.

FRENCHY
Oui, I will get branches for the fire. What will you cook?

COOKIE
Horse meat stew. With vegetable and something special.

TIMOTHY MACROY
What's that?

COOKIE
I throw in horse's rider to give it nice flavor. ha, ha, ha,
You like? OK I just joking... only saddle! ha, ha, ha,

BIG BEN
Cookie, you are a somethin' else. A funny China man.

COOKIE
Very funny. Yes, ha, ha. Frenchy! you put fire in wood for me? Yes?

FRENCHY
It's already done, Monsieur Wu.

John comes walking through camp.

JOHN MACROY
Listen up! Give an ear, this is important. The sun is setting, get your
bunks set up. Get chow and we'll get an early start in the mornin'.

TIMOTHY MACROY
What time?

JOHN MACROY
Sun up lad. The wee crack of dawn. Now eat up,and get some sleep.
EVERYONE remember, I promise $500 to the first
cowpoke that finds the entrance to this fantastic place.
The Land of the Dinosaurs!

BIG BEN
Good Lord, that be a years wages in one day. That sho'do
beat the five dollar winnin's for bare knuckle fightin'.

JUAN BARTELLI
It is good, Si?

FRENCHY
Mona me. Don't be talking about Frenchy's money. You will
be beaucoup jealous. Begging me for some green stuff.

EVERETTE KIRBY
What are you going to do if a Indian finds it? Cry?

BIG BEN
He's gonna be this black man's best friend in a Alabama minute.

TEX LAWSON
Aw, just trade him some blankets and beef jerky,
he'll give you that cash in a Texas second.

Tim walks over to Professor Perkins.

TIMOTHY MACROY
Hi professor.

PROFESSOR PERKINS
Hello Timothy.

TIMOTHY MACROY
Can I ask you a question?

PROFESSOR PERKINS
Sure. What is your question?

TIMOTHY MACROY
Do you have any ideas how this place could transfer
dinosaurs from 100 million years ago to today in 1880?

PROFESSOR PERKINS
Well Tim, there must be some tear in the universe
as we know it. This tear must have some type of
time travel, but I guess we'll find out.

TIMOTHY MACROY
It's kinda' scary...in a way, but really interesting in another way.

PROFESSOR PERKINS
I'd give anything to just bring back a skeleton or two.
Even a live Dinosaur egg. These are worth their weight
in gold. I'd really have a name for myself in history.

TIMOTHY MACROY
I guess?! I'd just like to see one with my own eyes. Maybe
we could capture a small one and bring it back?

PROFESSOR PERKINS
Now that would be to die for.

Cookie walks over to them.

COOKIE
Mister Tim, yo fadda' looks for you ova' da'.

He points to the other wagon.

TIMOTHY MACROY
Nice talking to you Professor Perkins. I have
to go. See you in the morning.

PROFESSOR PERKINS
Yes Tim, See you in the morning.

They depart. Tim goes to his father and Miss Deven. Professor Perkins
heads to the light by the other campfire to see what's going on?

JOHN MACROY
Well my love, how did you like my auto
feed dinosaur gun demonstration?

VIRGINIA DEVEN
Kinda' hard to shoot wafers out of the air.

JOHN MACROY
But man does not live by wafers alone my sweetness.
Ha, Ha. I believe it says that in the "Good Book".

VIRGINIA DEVEN
No, John it was "By bread alone", but it was a powerful
demonstration. A big gun can come in handy sometimes.

She winks and He smiles as large as life. Tim arrives.

JOHN MACROY
I was beginnin' to worry about ya' lad. It's your bedtime.
We've got a big day ahead on the 'morrow.

VIRGINIA DEVEN
It's good you came over Tim. I've got a smaller caliber six shooters
and holster that if your Dad says OK, I'd love to give to you.

TIMOTHY MACROY
That would be swell! Dad could I...please!

JOHN MACROY
Well, I don't know. Would ya' get some dog gone slumber
if I say yes? I mean keep it here with me 'till tomorrow
when Miss Deven can show you how to use it.

TIMOTHY MACROY
You've got my word! Oh thank you Miss Deven. Thanks Dad!

TIMOTHY MACROY (VO)
I remember thinking, hell if Dad didn't marry her, I
would! Those six shooters would come in handy.

He goes over and hugs her; she kisses him on the forehead.

JOHN MACROY
And don't forget your father.

He goes over and hugs him and gives a kiss.

JOHN MACROY
(cont)
Now get to bed youngin'.

He heads for the wagon. Meanwhile, Professor Perkins arrives at the campfire lit poker game. It's an open game of "Five Card Draw". They're playing for pocket change right now. The pot is full of nickels and dimes. Everette is dealing.

EVERETTE KIRBY
Get along little doggie! ok, read 'em and weep.
Do ya want a card and how many?... Ben?

He looks to see only a pair of queens.

BIG BEN
Brother Ben takes three cards and I sho' do like the ladies.

EVERETTE KIRBY
One, two and three.

Ben holds up his new hand- triple queens with an eight and a jack.

EVERETTE KIRBY
And you Frenchy?

He has two pairs - Jacks and tens.

                        FRENCHY
            This lousy hand. Everette just give me one
                 card. I might get another pair.

                     EVERETTE KIRBY
                There you be Mr. Par-ee.(Paris)

He looks at his hand and it is now a full house- Jacks full of tens.

And you Gaucho Jose?

He has ace, two, three, four, King.

                      JOSE LAGANA
        One card. Chica ...Cinco por favor.(small please..a five)

                     EVERETTE KIRBY
                   And one chica for you.

                      JOSE LAGANA
                      Gracias.(thanks)

Jose looks and he got a five. Having no poker face he smiles and
laughs over his straight.

                     EVERETTE KIRBY
                   Juan, how many cards.

He looks at his hand and he has a pair of deuces.

                      JUAN BARTELLI
                     I'll take three cards.

                     EVERETTE KIRBY
                Uno, dos, tres. (one, two, three)

Juan looks ever so slowly as his fanning reveals an ace, a six, and a nine.

JUAN BARTELLI
Santa Maria! (Holy Mary)

He throws His cards and folds.

EVERETTE KIRBY
Now if you will excuse me. I'll look at my cards first...

He has five, six, seven, eight of hearts and an ace of spades.

EVERETTE KIRBY
(cont)
I'll just discard one card and take one card like so.

His new card is the four of hearts which makes a straight flush. He looks disgusted. He looks at Ben.

EVERETTE KIRBY
Looks like you open the betting big Ben.

BIG BEN
Ben bets two quarters.

EVERETTE KIRBY
And you Frenchy ?

FRENCHY
I will raise... to one dollar.

The players grumble.

EVERETTE KIRBY
And you Jose?

JOSE LAGANA
It is mucho dinero (a lot of money),a days
wages. Lo ciento.(I'm sorry) He folds.

EVERETTE KIRBY
Well Frenchy...(long pause) I'm going to see
your dollar... and raise you two dollars.

The players gasp.

EVERETTE KIRBY
(cont)
The betting is to you Ben.

BIG BEN
Momma didn't raise no fool.

He folds

EVERETTE KIRBY
And you Frenchy?

FRENCHY
You are bluffing... you do not fool me! Here is the two more dollars.
Now what do you have... it can not beat my full house.

He shows jacks over tens -FULL HOUSE .

EVERETTE KIRBY
Oh I've got a flush...

FRENCHY
Good now show me and give me the money.

He reaches for the pot.

EVERETTE KIRBY
Not so fast...it's a straight flush.

he uncovers 4,5,6,7,and 8 of hearts.

FRENCHY
You cheated! Slight of hand.

EVERETTE KIRBY
Frenchy, I never cheat.

PROFESSOR PERKINS
I've been observing very closely, Monsieur La Rue, I
don't believe he cheated. Can we play again? I would
love to play a hand with you gentleman.

FRENCHY
Oui, and this time Ben is the dealer.

Everette rakes in his pot. Professor Perkins finds a seat.

BIG BEN
Every one ante up twenty five cents for da' pot.

They all ante.

PROFESSOR PERKINS
And there is my ante.

BIG BEN
So now you each get cards. Five of 'dem.

He deals five cards to each player. The last card he deals to himself.
They all look at their hands for cards to keep.

BIG BEN
(cont)
You ready Frenchy? How many cards?

He looks at a pair of deuces, a jack, a nine,and a five. He keeps the deuces.

FRENCHY
Give me three good cards, Monsieur.

He gets a seven, a four and a three. He has only a pair of Deuces. He becomes quiet.

BIG BEN
And you JO-SE? How many?

He looks at a pair of kings, an ace, a jack, and a three.

JOSE LAGANA
Give me. uno mas por favor (one more please)

BIG BEN
'Dat means one right? Here you go.

He picks it up and slowly fans his cards. He now has three kings and shakes his head.

BIG BEN
(cont)
Hows about you, Juan ?

He has only a pair of eights.

JUAN BARTELLI
I'll take three good cards por favor (please)

BIG BEN
There you is? Three.

He fans his cards with a deuce, two eights, a jack,and a ten. He quietly puts his cards down.

BIG BEN
And now it's your turn, Professor. How many cards does you need?

He briefly looks at his hand. It's a pair of fours, a queen, a three, and a five.

PROFESSOR PERKINS
I don't want any! I have a perfect hand for five cards.

Everyone looks a little taken back and wonders what he has.

BIG BEN
OK 'den. I guess it be your turn Everette.
How many cards does you...

Everette is quick to reply holding a pair of aces and a pair of eights.

EVERETTE KIRBY
One card, Big Ben, and make this winning hand even better.

BIG BEN
One card it is. Here you be.

He discards a jack and gains a nine. He remains aces and eights.

EVERETTE KIRBY
Thank you, I can see that money flashin' in my pockets right now!

BIG BEN
Now we open the betting and yo's first Frenchy.

FRENCHY
I'll pass.

BIG BEN
Oh. And you Jose?

JOSE LAGANA
I give twenty-five cents.

He throws in a quarter.

BIG BEN
Juan?

JUAN BARTELLI
I fold.

BIG BEN
Professor are you...

PROFESSOR PERKINS
I'll see the twenty-five and raise a dollar.

Everyone gasps. Everette, still confident, responds.

EVERETTE KIRBY
Well professor...you've been studyin' a little more
than Dinosaurs at that school of yours. OK. I see
your dollar and raise you two more dollars.

The group is quieted. Jose folds and the Professor responds.

PROFESSOR PERKINS
Let's raise it another ten dollars. You can't beat five
cards that make a hand. I saw your face when you got
your last card. The best you can do is two pairs.

Everette is showing nerves. He sweats, turns flushed in the face, and starts flicking his cards. The professor is calm. He looks at Everette with piercing eyes that would convince a righteous man he was going to hell.

EVERETTE KIRBY
OHH! I'm foldin' my Aces and eights.I know
you got your flush or a straight.

PROFESSOR PERKINS
Push the pot over.

The pot moves to him. He uncovers his hand.

PROFESSOR PERKINS
(cont)
Only a pair of fours...with a winning bet. Bluffing
is part of the game my good man.

They restrain Everette lunging for the Professor.

EVERETTE KIRBY
You lousy piece of cow shit, I oughta'...

PROFESSOR PERKINS
What, try and kill me because you folded a winning
hand?! "Life is full of surprises. Be prepared!"

The commotion draws John McRoy over to the card game.

JOHN MACROY
Gents, it'll be early when we rise. Lets forget the cards
and get a wee bit of sleep 'fore the sun's up.

BIG BEN
I'm with you Mister McRoy fo' somebody kills
someone over paper cards and paper money.

The game breaks and the players disperse.

JOHN MACROY
It looks like the professor found his way
into the cowboy's card game.

FRENCHY
And left with their money. Ha,ha, It serves Everette
right to lose a big pot. It's his turn to cry.

JOHN MACROY
I just don't want men with hard feelings if you know what
I mean. Libel to shoot one another. Oh... I've seen it!

FRENCHY
Good night, Sir.

JOHN MACROY
Get some shut-eye.

TIMOTHY MACROY (VO)
The professor was my teacher. I just didn't
see it coming. Not many did.

John walks back to Virginia.

VIRGINIA DEVEN
So what was that all about?

JOHN MACROY
A poker dispute, And of all things the professor
won and Everette was miffed.

VIRGINIA DEVEN
Why is that peculiar?

JOHN MACROY
I don't recall ever seeing Everette lose. The professor
must really be somethin'...when it comes to cards.

VIRGINIA DEVEN
And maybe when it comes to other things?!

Everyone turns in for the night with lone campfires burning.

EXT PLAINS NEAR THE BLACK HILLS - CONTINUOUS
-DAY BREAK

Cookie clanks a triangular breakfast bell to announce daybreak and
breakfast.

COOKIE
Come and get it. Breakfast is ready. You want eggs and
coffee and biscuits. Chop, Chop. Everybody eat too fast
and we go. Mister MacRoy say. Very fast we eat.

TIMOTHY MACROY (VO)
The morning clamor of metal coffee cups and
plates being filled with food was heard throughout
the camp.It smelled great! Everyone was
(MORE)

TIMOTHY MACROY (VO) (cont'd)
waking up to get their share of heaven.

JOHN MACROY
Good mornin' Everette and you Frenchy, , Big Ben,
Professor and Jose. How's the coffee and vittles?

JOSE LAGANA
Muy bien! (Very good!)

BIG BEN
Just what the Doctor ordered Sir. I be eatin' my way to my best,
'cause I'm findin' the passage way that makes the BIG money.

FRENCHY
Eat all you want my big friend. It will take
more than food to get you there.

Painted Horse walks over to the group and looks for Everette. John figures it out.

JOHN MACROY
Your looking for other white man this tall?

He shakes his head in agreement. The other two Sioux braves come over to join him.

JOHN MACROY
(cont)
Everette! I need your services over here.

He comes over from the other side of the wagon.

EVERETTE KIRBY
Yes boss, What can I do for ya'?

JOHN MACROY
Can you interpret what Painted Horse has to say.

EVERETTE KIRBY
No problem.

He turns toward the Sioux Braves,And speaks to them in their Lakota tongue.

EVERETTE KIRBY
(cont)
Tell me Painted Horse, what are you sensing?

PAINTED HORSE
The place where the beast appeared is a pony
ride to that small hill over there.

He points.

EVERETTE KIRBY
Boss he said the creature attacked him
where that small hill is over there.

JOHN MACROY
Alright then,lets get packed up and move there. FINISH UP! We're
moving' out! Everette tell him and the other Sioux to lead the way.

There is a lot of clamor as everyone races to throw their food down
and find the magical passage.

EXT UPPER PLAINS OF BLACK HILL-DAY CONTINUOUS

The wagons and people on horseback spread out following the
Indians. They approach the place where "BLUE WOLF" and the
beast vanished. For some reason the horses are on edge?
They're easily spooked. Painted Horse feels the spirit of BLUE
WOLF. He closes his eyes and chants. The wagons and horses stop.

PAINTED HORSE
I hear you my brother. Show us the way. Our Great Fathers and
Chiefs past, make us to see the path. Gift us with this knowledge.

The group is on horseback and walking.

JOHN MACROY
Spread out lads! It's around here somewhere.

Ben walks near some tall grass and sees something. Red liquid was oozing from the soil.

BIG BEN
I found sometin'!

Others look at the blood red liquid. Someone else sees the air moving in sections like heat rising from the desert.

FRENCHY
Look at the air!

He reaches forward near the disturbance. His hand disappears and returns. I found it! Sacre blue ! It is here!

BIG BEN
Yous means...we found it.

FRENCHY
Oui, Big Ben,we found it.

John rides up dismounts and gives a look.

JOHN MACROY
What did you find?

BIG BEN
Give a look see Mister MacRoy. Frenchy do it again.

Frenchy puts his hand through the time warp.

FRENCHY
Ahhhh! Something's got my arm! Help!

He screams violently. Three people rush to his aid. John is one of them. Frenchy pulls his hand back out smirking.

FRENCHY
Just having fun with you. I guess I split the $500
with Ben? Oui, Monsouer McRoy?

JOHN MACROY
That's affirmative Frenchy.

He pulls out a bankroll.

JOHN MACROY
(cont)
$250 for you Frenchy and $250 for you Ben.

FRENCHY
Mona Me. Frenchy's liking this trip already.

BIG BEN
It sho' do look fine to me also. My, my, my.

Ben kisses the money, puts it in a pouch, then slides it in his pocket.

John puts his hand through the same hole in time and it disappears. He feels a plant and yanks out a frond.

JOHN MACROY
Would you look at that?!

The professor gets down from the wagon and runs to them.

PROFESSOR PERKINS
John let me see that if you would, please.

He hands him the leaf and the professor inspects it with a magnifying lens.

PROFESSOR PERKINS
(cont)
It's just what I thought! It's a
Williamsonia, a form of cycadophyte!

TEX LAWSON
And what in the hell is that.

PROFESSOR PERKINS
It's triceratops favorite food.
It went extinct with the dinosaurs.

Painted Horse gets closer with his fellow Sioux.

PAINTED HORSE
(In Lakota)
Now is the time. Our ancestors are with us let us
enter and find my brother BLUE WOLF.

JOHN MACROY
Hold on there, lets...

The three braves mount their painted ponies and ride into the abyss.

JOHN MACROY
(cont)
Damn it the hell! Let's line up the wagons and horses. Follow
them in, I say. Don't get separated! Do it now! Hurry it up men!

EVERETTE KIRBY
John, the Souix went in to find BLUE WOLF. We have
to stick together. And get our fire power out.

JOHN MACROY
Good thinking, Ben find a good place to tie up the
wagon and horses, then get out the rifles.

VIRGINIA DEVEN
John I'm going in with you and Tim.

JOHN MACROY
You bet my love, LET'S DO IT NOW! Quickly
afore the damned entrance closes up.

EXT CRETACEOUS PERIOD JUNGLE AND PLAINS
SETTING-DAY

They all manage to enter. The last wagon goes into the entrance with
their dog barking out the back of the wagon. Timothy records it in
his diary.

TIMOTHY MACROY (VO)
"Thursday, July 10th, 1890 at 10:30 AM we entered this lost
land of the dinosaurs. I hope we live to talk about it."
I remember that entry very well. Living to talk
about it is the most difficult part.

JOHN MACROY
OK, You cowpokes bring the wagons and horses over there
in that glen of trees. We need to make some plans.

EVERETTE KIRBY
Boss if I could say somethin ' here. Let's stay to the
outside of those trees to avoid an ambush. We have
more room for a quick get-away if need be.

JOHN MACROY
Good thinking. Wait! Stop the wagons.Look up in that tree.

The three Sioux ride in to greet the wagons at that moment It was a
Sioux arrow shot into the trunk. The three Sioux braves ride up on
their ponies.

JOHN MACROY
Everette ! Talk with these savages and find out about the arrow.

They ride over to Everette and talk.

EVERETTE KIRBY
They say it is BLUE WOLF's arrow. He
marked the tree to find his way back.
They have yet to find him.

While they talk a terrific roar shakes the grassland and forest.

DINOSAURS
RRRROOOARRRR!

TEX LAWSON
Awww shi-i-t!

JOHN MACROY
Get your guns ready boys.
Ben break open those dinosaur guns!

BIG BEN
I be doin' it for you can say black-eyed peas.

He drags the crates from the wagon and pries them open with a crowbar. His eyes are as big as saucers. Big Ben is scared.

BIG BEN
(cont)
Here be three rifles with ammo Mister McRoy.

JOHN MACROY
Ben you take one, give one to Miss Deven
and I'll take one of those beauties.

BIG BEN
Don't forget Mister McRoy we have two
more crates of guns and ammo.

JOHN MACROY
I'll be savin' those near the end of the safari.
It's a little insurance policy.

BIG BEN
I hears ya'.

The professor walks over to John from the wagon he has a crazed look.

PROFESSOR PERKINS
Greetings John, Amazing stuff! We are in the Cretaceous
Period from all that I've studied. We must look out for Flying
dinosaurs like the Pteradactyl and the Pteradon. They would
see us from the sky and could out maneuver us; even eat us.

JOHN MACROY
Hungry eagles are they?

PROFESSOR PERKINS
Yes with a head as big as a man and wings forty foot wide.
The real danger on land will be from Tyrannosaurus
Rex. The largest hunting carnivore to have walked the
Dakotas. He could out run us and cause havoc.

Tex rides closer to hear .

TEX LAWSON
Did you say that there's s
pre-historic flying dinosaur that could eat this Texan?

PROFESSOR PERKINS
That's what we've found studying
fossils or bones of past creatures.

TEX LAWSON
Damn! If that over sized flyin' horny toad tries that
with me, I'm gonna rope him ,tie 'em to a
prehistoric tree and shoot his ass!

EVERETTE KIRBY
I'm with ya' on that one Tex.

Virginia rides closer to John.

VIRGINIA DEVEN
John, there you are, dear.
What is the plan? What are we doing?

JOHN MACROY
Missy... I think we need to search for BLUE
WOLF and if on the way we run into a nasty
creature, it be time to try out our fire power.

VIRGINIA DEVEN
I think we'd have a better chance in finding him if we
broke into two groups and met back at this tree.

They look up to see the arrow stuck high in the trunk. They form two
teams with two wagons to search on either side of the jungle glen.

JOHN MACROY
Listen up mates! We're splitn' up into two teams. One team
will explore to the right of this glen of trees and the other
team to the left. We'll meet back here tonight for dinner.

EVERETTE KIRBY
Where abouts are we meeting tonight?

JOHN MACROY
This here tree with the arrow is our meeting place.
Everette you and the professor pick your guys.

Everette, know that I, Miss Deven, and Tim are on your wagon team.
Professor you pick three people to go with you and your wagon.

PROFESSOR PERKINS
Ben, Frenchy, and Cookie.

JOHN MACROY
Aye, that's hittin' below the belt pickin', Cookie. OK, we're taking
Juan, Cause he can also cook, when of course we divide up the food.

FRENCHY
What about the Souix braves?

They looked around and they were gone.

VIRGINIA DEVEN
Well it looks like we've got three teams now: Cowboy
team #1, Cowboy team #2, and the Indians.

TEX LAWSON
Aw hell! It ain't fun unless it's cowboys and Indians with
a few dinosaurs thrown in for a little ex-cite-ment.

Young Tim walks over to his Dad and Virginia.

TIMOTHY MACROY
Dad, I heard we're drawing teams?

JOHN MACROY
You don't have to worry a bit son,
you're with Miss Deven and me.

TIMOTHY MACROY
Good I'll get my stuff and move to your wagon.

JOHN MACROY
Would you do it quickly, laddie?!

EVERETTE KIRBY
Tex, you're goin' on our team.

TEX LAWSON
Thank Ye kindly.

He takes out his lariat and shows off his skills at lassoing a small tree stump while on horseback.

TEX LAWSON
(cont)
I won't disappoint ya.

PROFESSOR PERKINS
OK I guess that leaves Jose, you're on our team.

Jose looks back at Juan and reluctantly heads toward Frenchy's team.

PROFESSOR PERKINS
(cont.)
Before we head out, John, I think you should evenly
spread out the guns and ammo. We all need the
fire power in case something goes wrong.

JOHN MACROY
Alright, Ben get the other
crate of dinosaur guns and ammo and put it on their wagon.

BIG BEN
Sir. It already be there.

JOHN MACROY
Right you are. OK men, get a move on it. Find BLUE
WOLF and meet back here tonight at the arrow tree.

The wagons and cowpoke head out their different ways.

TIMOTHY MACROY (VO)
I felt good being with Dad and Virginia. Dad was very smart,
and Virginia was not only a great shot, but her savvy was
brilliant. We were about to need all of that...and more.

The wagons veer in different directions. The Professor's wagon on glen
to the left of the strip of jungle and Everette's wagon to the right of
the trees. Soon they were out of sight of one another. The Professor's
wagon approaches a watering hole. A prehistoric swampy area.

FRENCHY
Would you look at that!

Everyone slows to look. It is an assortment of giant herbavores;
Triceratops, Parasaurolophi, duck-billed Corythosaurus, and other
different dinosaurs dotting the herd.

PROFESSOR PERKINS
They'll put me in Washington, DC. In my own
office. Wealthy and distinguished.

Everyone peers at the prehistoric herd with utter amazement.

COOKIE
We get away chop,chop... or ma ma
comes to get us for babies.

BIG BEN
Ya she be protectin' those babies alright!

COOKIE
No not protect, she get us for food for babies.

The crazed professor interjects.

PROFESSOR PERKINS
Let's get closer. Possibly we can
distract them and steal some eggs?

FRENCHY
Sacre Bleau! Professor! We don't want to
exchange our lives for a dinosaur egg!?

The professor pulls out a gun and points it in their faces.

PROFESSOR PERKINS
Well, for openers, let's hand over your revolvers
and the $250 dollars you each won for finding
this place. You first, Frenchy, then Ben.

Frenchy hands Professor Perkins his pistol and the money, but hides
his Bowie knife.

FRENCHY
You are not a professor, I knew when you played your bluff in
poker. You are a professional flimflam man. A fraud. Who are you?

PROFESSOR PERKINS
Now you Ben, I'll take that $250 and the pistol.

He points the revolver to his nose as Ben hands his gun and fishes for the pouch in his pocket.

BIG BEN
You are as low as they go.

He takes the money while pointing the pistol.

PROFESSOR PERKINS
You didn't believe I was a professor, Frenchy? Damned
good...no I was incarcerated in Colorado Penitentary
when Professor Perkins paid our wonderful facility
a visit. I became professor Perkins and he
became... well, me... Randall Starks, a dead man.

FRENCHY
So you killed him and became the Professor!?

PROFESSOR PERKINS
Exactly...You are a smart bunch. My real dad was a learned
man; a college grad'. He made sure we were educated and it
came in handy. I read about dinosaurs every chance I could.

BIG BEN
I hope one of dem' giant lizards eats yo' educated ass.

FRENCHY
I hope he eats it slowly.

PROFESSOR PERKINS
Now that's not nice boys. You are the ones that have to
worry about getting yourselves eaten. You see, I want you to
go over to that herd...and bag me some dinosaur eggs.

He points to a mound of mud and fern leaves 12 feet high and about
100 feet from the water.

PROFESSOR PERKINS
(cont.)
See that mound of dirt and leaves. That is where the eggs are.
Get some buckets from Cookie and when you get there, fill it
with a little of the dirt and leaves from the nest. I want a cluster
of eggs in each bucket and you might live to see tomorrow.

FRENCHY
You Get the eggs, so what are you going to do
then professor? or should I say Randall?

PROFESSOR PERKINS
Professor is still good, because I am going to hook up with PT
Barnum. The public will see the first dinosaurs born 100 million
years after extinction. The dinosaurs will grow to great heights and
so will my wallet. I didn't study the professor's research for nothing.

BIG BEN
I'd watch out if I were you, 'cause it's just a matter
of time 'fore 'da trut' comes forward.

PROFESSOR PERKINS
By that time I will have all the money I need to live
comfortably by a different name, in another place in the
world. NOW GET GOING AND GET THOSE EGGS!!

They leave the wagon and circle around the herd with a bucket in
hand. The herd is grazing and not paying attention to their advances.

FRENCHY
Listen to me, men. This guy is going to kill us whether we get
these eggs or not. Let's approach the nest and run for the trees
as fast as we can. We can cut through the trees to McRoy.

BIG BEN
What about Cookie?

FRENCHY
He's not dumb, believe me. Chinamen are some
of the smartest people I know. He will find a way.
We have to strike while the iron is hot.

JOSE LAGANA
Si, we must do it now. We may not get another chance.

BIG BEN
I'm with ya' my brothers.

FRENCHY
Ok. On the count of three run like hell
to those trees. One, two, three!

They drop their buckets and take off. Frenchy and Jose are at the
front and Ben is bringing up the rear.

PROFESSOR PERKINS
Why you dirty sons of bitches! I'm going
to have to shoot your asses.

He runs to get the dinosaur gun from the wagon. The gun is loaded
and he commences to fire.

PROFESSOR PERKINS
This is what you get for double crossin' me.

Blam!, Blam!, Blam!, Blam!, Blam! the rounds explode toward the
men, chasing them in a strafing pattern from left to right. Frenchy
and Jose make it into the trees. Ben is thirty feet behind and bullets
are almost catching him.

FRENCHY
Come on Ben you can make it!

JOSE LAGANA
Rapido Ben, Come on!

A bullet catches Ben in the calf muscle bringing him down.

BIG BEN
I'm hit! You boys jus' leave me.Get otta here
as fast as you can. Don't be stupid.

FRENCHY
You're the stupid one if you think
we're leaving our friend behind.

He low crawls to Ben and Jose is waiting behind a tree. Ben is dragged
to safety.

BIG BEN
I still think you all should leave ol' Ben be...

FRENCHY
If you don't shut up about that you're gonna
get tied up and dragged to the wagon.

BIG BEN
OK. I hears ya'.

FRENCHY
Now I still have this (Bowie Knife) and this is
what i'm going to do for my good buddy.

He takes off his undershirt and cuts a bandage ties up his wound.

BIG BEN
That feels real good. The bleedin' is not so much now.

FRENCHY
And you're going to need something to help keep up. Stand
up Ben on your other good leg and against the tree.

He takes his knife and cuts a "Y" shaped sapling armpit height. He
wraps some more under shirt around the top for comfort.

FRENCHY
Now don't say Frenchy never gave you anything. You have a
bandage and a crutch. Now you will travel faster than all of us.

BIG BEN
And two good friends.

JOSE LAGANA
We need to get out of here muy pronto. LOOK!

The Professor is forcing Cookie to collect dinosaur eggs at gunpoint.

PROFESSOR PERKINS
And Cookie don't be dumb, like running for the
woods like the others, If you want to live.

COOKIE
I'll get your dinosaur eggs. Don't worry.

PROFESSOR PERKINS
Good. We understand one another.

Cookies leaves with a bucket in hand. He gets to the nest by carefully
inching his way closer without disturbing the mothers. Back at the
wagon, the professor watches Cookie intently, not seeing the two
giant snakes that intend on making the team of horses a meal. The
horses sense their presence and start to throw a fit.

PROFESSOR PERKINS
What the...?

One of the snakes raises up fourteen feet like a giant cobra. These prehistoric reptiles have remnants of front and back feet. The Other snake raises up also.

PROFESSOR PERKINS
(cont)Hell's bells!

He raises his large rifle ever so intently,and he pulls the trigger. THE CLIP JAMS!

PROFESSOR PERKINS
(cont)
For the love of Mike!

He pulls it out and runs for the wagon for a new clip. The snakes pursue at a fast pace.

PROFESSOR PERKINS
You are not...going to ...get... me!

The horses rear up and wildly fight for their lives.In the distance, Cookie finds his cue to drop the bucket and run for the trees.

COOKIE
I gotta' find Frenchy.

He fights through the jungle to find the others. The Professor arrives at the wagon, rapidly loads the fresh clip, turns and fires. Snakes explode in pieces as multiple rounds hit them. BLAM! BLAM! BLAM! BLAM! BLAM! BLAM!

PROFESSOR PERKINS
Take this, Lucifer! One and two!

The horses continue to spook. The gunfire causes the herd of dinosaurs to stampede in a large moving circle. The stampeding Dinosaurs suddenly part like the Red Sea in two directions revealing their fears. Two giant "T" Rex stand roaring in the center.

PROFESSOR PERKINS
Oh Crap!

There's utter confusion.ROARR! ROARR! The first "T" Rex snatches a duck-billed dinosaur from the stampede and shakes his head tearing it limb by limb. The other "T" Rex puts it snout in the air. He smells the dying snakes.

PROFESSOR PERKINS
Come here boy! That's it.

The Professor mounts a horse from the team and and releases the rest of the wagon team. He gallops away with "T" Rex on his tail. The dinosaur is closing. The professor hits the horse to get it to go faster.

PROFESSOR PERKINS
Come on , Damn it.Times a wastin'

"T" Rex snaps again grabbing part of the horses tail. Professor turns the horse to face the adversary and opens fire. The horse rears up and drops the professor and takes off. The wounded "T" Rex limps toward his adversary to do damage. The professor quickly picks up the rifle and gets a bead on "T" Rex.

PROFESSOR PERKINS
Come on, Gimpy! Try eating this!

Bam! Bam! Bam! The huge dino gets ten feet from him with flesh popping everywhere a bullet hits. He crumbles into a ball of wounded dinosaur meat. The professor walks over nonchalantly and finishes the creature in the heart. Bam!,Bam! Blood flies everywhere.

PROFESSOR PERKINS
No... I'm the King!

In the distance the Cleidsdales rampage pulling a disintegrating wagon behind them. The professor sees a lone "T" Rex in pursuit.

PROFESSOR PERKINS
That "T" bastard! I need those horses.

Out of the corner of his eye he spots the horse that threw him. It's near the trees. He walks slowly to him as he calls.

PROFESSOR PERKINS
Here boy. Good boy, come here. It's ok. I'll take good care of you.

The horse comes closer. It follows the edge of the trees. It is getting calmer and relaxes as it bobs his head with every deliberate trot. It knows it's safe and relaxes as it is within 30feet of the professor.

RRROOAARRRR! CRUNCH!CRUNCH! In a split second a "T" Rex darts from the edge of the trees to kill and devour the horse.

PROFESSOR PERKINS
This really pisses me off!

He gets his gun together. Puts in a new clip. The "T" Rex stops, then drops the horse and charges.The professor sings a song in between rifle bursts.

PROFESSOR PERKINS
(cont) I, BLAM! wish you a Merry, BLAM! BLAM! Christmas, BLAM!,BLAM!and a Happy!BLAM!, BLAM!,BLAM!. New Year!

He walks over to the crumpling dinosaur and put the last killing slug in his heart. BLAM!!

PROFESSOR PERKINS
(cont)Gosh I love the holidays.
Now Cookie! Where did you go?!

EXT GLEN TO THE RIGHT OF THE JUNGLE- MCROY'S COMPANY- DAY

The other wagon has gone about three miles from the arrow tree.

The open area is soon decorated with huge fifty foot trees that look like a cross between a palm tree and a fern with hanging moss. The open land starts shrinking to semi-jungle. Small flying dinosaurs are startled from the trees as they approach.In the disance a RROOARRRR! is heard. Flying reptiles leave the trees by the hundreds.The sky is full of their high pitched shrieks as they block the sun. The RROOOAAARRRR! is heard again as "T" Rex moves closer. The swarms of high pitched cries are broken by a low dull WAANK!

WAANK! WAANK! screech and SNAP! Two large pteradactyls fly through the swarms picking off victims with one gulp. They were like fory foot pelicans diving in a sea of anchovies.

JOHN MACROY
Would you look at that. It's like a huge
flying bat with a beak like a stork.

VIRGINIA DEVEN
I don't know what it is, but I don't trust....

Just then the Pteracactyl turns and sees the dog walking behind the wagon.

EVERETTE KIRBY
Look out! He's comin' right at us!!!

John quickly reacts lifting his dinosaur gun as the flying monster descends.WHAM!, WHAM!,WHAM!, WHAM!,WHAM!. THE GREAT FLYING BEAST FALLS APART AS THE ROUNDS EXPLODE. Tex and Everette also fire six shooters.

EVERYONE
Wahoo! Yipee! We got'em !

The Dino-bird rolls into a pile of wings and bloody body parts and stops in front of the the dog. He shakes in fear but manages to get out a pathetic scolding. Bark!, Bark! He then goes and hides beneath the wagon.

TIMOTHY MACROY
Come up here "Tuffy". Get in the wagon.

TEX LAWSON
I think Tuffy's name should be "Damned lucky."

EVERETTE KIRBY
Or maybe "Scared Tuffless".

JOHN MACROY
Look gents, we said we'd meet back at the arrow
tree at 6:00 PM and it is about 4:00 PM now We
haven't made contact with the Indians and...

TIMOTHY MACROY
Dad, I forgot to tell you...

JOHN MACROY
Not now Son.

TIMOTHY MACROY
But Dad,

VIRGINIA DEVEN
John let's hear what Tim has to say. It could be important.

JOHN MACROY
Son...for the love of Mike, what is it?

TIMOTHY MACROY (VO)
My Dad could be so bull headed at times. It
was easier dealing with a jack-ass.

TIMOTHY MACROY
Dad, some Mountain men in town showed me
how to tell how long ago animals passed by.

JOHN MAC ROY
How's that Lad?

TIMOTHY MAC ROY
You feel their scat. If it's warm with heat they
were here within the last ten minutes. If its barely
warm and still moist, a half hour and if it's cold with
good color it could have been 3-12 hours ago.

JOHN MAC ROY
So how were these.

TIMOTHY MAC ROY
I checked the horse droppings that weren't
ours and they were still warm.

TEX LAWSON
So they gotta' be right around the corner.

EVERETTE KIRBY
Hey! Look up at those trees. Arrows! One, two, three...

TEX LAWSON
Four, five, six, and seven. Looks like those
injuns ran into some trouble.

JOHN MACROY
Remember gents, they didn't miss ANY shot
against the six Pawnee braves.

TEX LAWSON
And look at all the different angles. Its as if
they circled a dinosaur on horseback!

EVERETTE KIRBY
And by the looks of the arrows path that something was huge.

JOHN MACROY
Well...let's call to them. They might hear us?!

He cups his hands together and belts out a call.

JOHN MACROY
(cont)Hello! Hello! Can you hear me?! Hello! Hello! (talking)
I guess they're out of range? Everette, call to them in Lakota.

He cups his hands.

EVERETTE KIRBY
Hoota! Hoota! Hoota!

JOHN MACROY
What are you saying?

EVERETTE KIRBY
Where are you? I guess they're outta' range.

You can hear loud roars and faint Indian war cries in the distance.

TEX LAWSON
Did you hear that? Listen!

VIRGINIA DEVEN
I can hear a roar then Indian cries.

Small images of dinosaurs surrounded by Indians on horseback. The images grow larger as the fight draws close.

TIMOTHY MACROY
Look! There they are!

The Indians chase a white triceratops while a "T" Rex circles. It stoops to roar and shake his head to scare back the Indians. They both want the same prize.

JOHN MACROY
Is that four Indians on 3 horses? Virginia could you
get my spy glass from the trunk in the wagon?

TIMOTHY MACROY
Dad, I'll get it!

He runs feverishly.

JOHN MACROY
Well, that boy is gone before I can give an answer.

He returns.

TIMOTHY MACROY
Here, Dad.

JOHN MACROY
Thanks, son.

He spies the scenery to find a fight to kill the albino triceratops.

VIRGINIA DEVEN
John, what do you see?

JOHN MACROY
Here love, give a look see. It's four Indians
trying to kill a white dinosaur and another
dinosaur is trying to kill it as well.

JOHN MACROY
(cont) Listen!

A wierd bellow and screach is followed by a RRROAARRR! The gound is rumbling. It feels like an earth quake. Then they see it coming right at them. It's the huge white triceratops followed by a "T" Rex and four indians on three horses.

JOHN MAC ROY
There they are! The Indians are with BLUE WOLF.

BLUE WOLF is doubled up on Stright Arrow's horse. He barks orders to the other Sioux warriors.

BLUE WOLF
(in Lakota tongue)

Stay with the White devil and kill him. Shoot for the eyes. When the walking lizard stops to eat him...we will kill them both.

EVERETTE KIRBY
Look John, It's BLUE WOLF with the rest of the Indians.

EVERYONE
Yahoo!

JOHN MACROY
Let's get those rifles out men. Get those
dinosaurs. Watch not to shoot an Indian.

TEX LAWSON
Hell, when I was in the Army, it was shoot the Indians
and watch that you don't kill any lizards.

EVERETTE KIRBY
These are our friends...kill the lizards.

TEX LAWSON
Just funnin'.

Roaring, snarling, hissing belching is mixed with Indian war cries.
The ground is trembling terribly as "T" Rex maneuvers to get advantage. John dismounts.

JOHN MACROY
Quick Everette, Help me get this rifle set up .

They put the barrel and the magazine onto the stock and trigger
assembly . Everette rapidly gives John an extra clip.

EVERETTE KIRBY
Attach this extra clip to your belt.

John takes position. The Indians are back and forth on horseback.
He can't get a clear shot.

JOHN MACROY
Everette, get closer and tell the Indians in
Lakota to stand clear of my big guns.

Everette rides closer,"T" rex turns and chases Everette out of the fray. He rides toward John and the other cowboys. The Indians concentrate on the white beast.

JOHN MACROY
(cont) Closer... men get ready... a little closer,
NOW! LET HIM HAVE IT! Blam!
Blam! Pow! POW! POW! POP! POP! POP!

The Giant "T"Rex is turning toward each adversary as his flesh is exploding from the gunfire. He finally looks at John as his worst opponent and makes a disabled charge. John is immovable filling him with all that he's got. He's seriously wounded but still coming. John runs out of ammo.

EVERETTE KIRBY
John, your clip on your belt! Your clip!

He can't hear. Virginia is calm on the outside but hysterical inside. She rides to John, but stops by the other cowboys.

VIRGINIA DEVEN
Someone give me a rifle, Quick.

TEX LAWSON
Here, but it ain't no dinosaur gun.

He throws and she catches on horseback. "T"rex is fifty feet from John, hobbling in when John steps wrong and goes down.

VIRGINIA DEVEN
Stay down John.

She rides side saddle and fires from horseback bullets flying. The horse causes her to miss too much. She dismounts with John and takes aim placing five rapid shots in the eyes. POW! POW! POW!

POW! POW! "T" Rex stiffins and falls like an axed tree toward the two of them.

JOHN MACROY

Let's move back woman!

They scramble. "T" Rex falls with a thunderous, BOOM! He misses them by inches and sprays his final breath all over them.

VIRGINIA DEVEN

Quickly John. We must head for the wagon.

JOHN MACROY

I'm goin' fast as I can, but me ankle is a wee bit out of sorts Missy.

VIRGINIA DEVEN

Hang on to me, John. W'ere gonna get out of here.

Everette rides over and gives interference with his rifle on horseback. The Indians have shot almost all of their arrows into the Triceratops, He is going strong. Tex Lawson jumps into the battle.

TEX LAWSON

Everette Cover me with one of those dinosaur guns.

He takes out his largest lariat rope and twirls the lasso overhead as he approaches the great albino dinosaur. He looks for something to tie into. He sees a rock with an armlike feature.

TEX LAWSON

(cont)It's time to do my magic. You can
snort all you want you white horny
toad. This is my rodeo and you are goin' down.

He rides alongside the galloping beast and the Indians give him room. He throws the lariat and it misses. Meanwhile, Jose cannot contain himself any longer. He mounts his horse with his bolas and twirls them overhead as he approaches the beast.

JUAN BARTELLI
Tex, I will try for his legs you get him with your rope.

TEX LAWSON
I hear ya.

They ride around the animal confusing it on their horses. The Indians weave in and out, but sense they must give them room.

JUAN BARTELLI
I'm goin in.

He twirls his bolas and releases at the dinosaur's ankles. The bolas wrap around and bring him to his knees like a rodeo bull.

TEX LAWSON
My turn.

He twirls the lasso and the white monster follows his
horse the bolla rope snaps, the beast gets up and aims his three giant horns at Tex and gallops toward his horse.

JUAN BARTELLI
Look out!

Juan is out of position to help.

The lariat goes around the animal's neck plate. Tex jumps from his horse and wraps the rope around an arm on the rock several times. The beast goes for the horse and all three horns take it down and the rope snaps. The horse dies.

TEX LAWSON
Aww shit! I loved that horse. I'll get him
for ya. Apache. He's gonna pay.

John appears on horseback.

JOHN MACROY
I've got a dinosaur gun and clips. Tex get out of here, quickly.

TEX LAWSON
No sir, Give me that dinosaur gun. I got to avenge my
horse. Apache ain't gonna die for nothin'. That big white
pile of prehistoric turds is goin. Man is he ever goin'.

JOHN MAC ROY
OK laddie, here. Now be careful.

John gives Tex the dinosaur gun. Tex walks deliberately with heavy
boot marks and a huge gun pointed at a charging Triceratops.

TEX LAWSON
(cont) Now clear out. That ghost beast is going down.

Tex waves the Indians off. The triceratops follows the Indians, but Tex
makes a lot of clamor and waves at the animal. It picks up speed and
concentrates on Tex alone. He opens fire. BLAM! BLAM! BLAM!
You can see the white dino' loaded with arrows. It closes on Tex. He
opens up machine gun style, and it's not stopping.

JOHN MACROY
You can't stop that thing!

John gets another dinosaur gun and limps quickly up to join him.

JOHN MACROY
Let's aim for the heart not the head.

TEX LAWSON
Got it!

They open up with some cowboys shooting as well. It's deafening.
BLAM! POP! BLAM! POP! POW! POW! BANG! BANG! POP!
POP! The creature comes straight at them and 20 feet away drops to
his knees, dies, but skids into John and Tex.

EVERYONE
Yeah! Wahooo!!! Yipee!!! Wahoo!!!!

The Indians get down from their horses and yelp and scream as they
dance around the beast. BLUE WOLF hugs Straight Arrow, smiles
and continues to dance. Virginia runs to John.

JOHN MACROY
Well, my love, we're good
for each other, no?

She puts her arms around him kisses him, and looks into his eyes.

VIRGINIA DEVEN
I am looking forward to being your
wife and Tim's new Mom.

Tim is running over and hugs them both.

TIMOTHY MACROY
I love you Dad, I love you Virginia. Let's go home!

TIMOTHY MACROY (VO)
Now that would have been wonderful. We leave,and it's
a storybook ending. The hero gets his woman, the boy
gets his new mom and the cowboys and Indians both win
over the dinosaurs! Wow...how life is full of surprizes.

JOHN MACROY
Leaving now sounds good to me, how about you guys.

TEX LAWSON
Lets go.

EVERETTE KIRBY
I'm with you.

JUAN BARTELLI
Yo Tambien! (Me too)

JOHN MACROY
Everybody give an ear. We got what we came for.
Possibly more than we bargained for, but what say you
if I pay each one a $200 bonus and let's go home.

EVERYONE
Horray! Yippee! Yahoo!

Everyone is celebrating. BLUE WOLF thanks John for killing the
Evil one. Everette interprets.

BLUE WOLF
I have been on the run in this land of monsters for five moons
without my horse. The White monster killed him. I knew the
Great Father heard my prayers. I also knew that my ancestors,
Thunder Sky and Quick Wind would lead someone to guide
me back. Thank you my Great White Hunter friend.

John grasps his hand with two of his. They shake their heads in smiles
and approval.

JOHN MACROY
Everette, tell BLUE WOLF that we are going
home to see his father, Red Eagle.

TEX LAWSON
Say boss, we better get back to the
arrow tree to meet the others.
We're late. But I was wonderin'.
Didn't we come here for a trophy?

JOHN MACROY
Are you thinking what I'm thinking?

TEX LAWSON
Let's cut the head off of that Tri cera thing and take it
back home. Hell people'd pay a lot just to see it.

JOHN MACROY
Let's do it!

TEX LAWSON
I get half of any money. We both took him down?!

JOHN MACROY
That you did Lad...It's a deal.

Tex and John go back to the beast and take a couple of hand saws.
They see the enormity of the task.

JOHN MACROY
Let's just saw off a couple of horns.

TEX LAWSON
I guess, but I wish we could mount
that head in Whiskey Creek Bar!

Juan is over by the stream shouting. He found something. He's jump-
ing up and down.

JUAN BARTELLI
Vamanos rapido.(Let's come here Quickly) Rapido
(Quickly) Oro, (gold) Mucho oro!.(Lots of gold!)

EVERETTE KIRBY
I know what that Spanish means...he found gold.

EXT JUNGLE STRIP OF TREES SEPARATING THE
WAGONS- DAY

Frenchy, Jose and Ben struggle through the thick vegetation to catch
up with the other wagon. Frenchy leads the way. Jose helps Ben to
limp quickly on his crutch.

BIG BEN
I'm sorry gents, Big Ben has got to rest for a
short spell. Is that alright Frenchy?

FRENCHY
It's just fine Ben. Catch your breath for a little....

JOSE LAGANA
Did you hear that?

FRENCHY
Hear what?

BIG BEN
Shhhh! I hears it too! It sound like Cookie!

Cookie shouts from the distance.

COOKIE
Ben! Frenchy! Can you hear me?

FRENCHY
I hear him... It is Cookie!

The group responds.

EVERYONE
Cookie, were over here. Come this way, follow our voices

COOKIE
I see you! I'm coming, chop, chop!

Cookie pulls and tugs through the vegetation and methodically makes his way toward the guys. Some of the tall palm trees have creatures clinging above the jungle floor. Cookie was not going unnoticed.

BIG BEN
Cookie, I hears you, but I can't see you.

One large camelion looking dinosaur about 10 feet in length is spiraling down a tree in Cookie's path. Frenchy decides to meet Cookie to help. He's made a make shift machete from his large Bowie knife to hack at the vegetation. Finally Frenchy meets up with Cookie.

FRENCHY
Good to see you my...

The huge lizard perched head down tail up on the tree above their head, shoots a huge sticky tongue onto Cookie like a camelion catching a cricket.

COOKIE
Help! Awf Ow! Help! French...y!

Frenchy jumps into action severing the lizard's tongue with one swipe of his knife. The lizard drops to the jungle floor in pain. Frenchy untangles Cookie from the sticky tongue remnant while the tree climbing dino writhes & convulses.

FRENCHY
Quick, Cookie, go to Ben and
Jose, I got to finish this beast.

Cookie runs to Ben & Jose. Meanwhile, Frenchy, jumps on the tongueless lizard stabs it repeatedly and wrestles it like an alligator. It soon lay lifeless. He cuts some meat off for a dinner meal and wraps it in a piece of his shirt.

BIG BEN
Frenchy! Are you alright? Frenchy!

Frenchy shouts back, then walks cautiously. He talks when he gets close.

FRENCHY
I'm alright. I had to kill the beast and cut off some
steaks for us. He didn't have much to
say...tongue tied I guess? Oui?

BIG BEN
You know Frenchy, ha, ha, you're gettin' funnier
than this good ole' Cookie here.

COOKIE
What's so funny? Lizard not know when
he attack a China man to eat him, other hungry men
see no more coffee, eggs & beans in their future. They
want good food, and kill lizard for Cookie.

EVERYONE
Ha,ha,ha!

FRENCHY
I think we should think of a plan, before we do anything else.

BIG BEN
I certainly agree with that.

JOSE LAGANA
Yo tambien, Me too.

FRENCHY
Maybe we should head to MacRoy's wagon right away? That crazy professor is on our tail and he's proven he can kill.

BIG BEN
I am with ya's, but I need to rest shortly,and I'll be o.k..

COOKIE
When I left the Professor, he was fighting off giant snakes and dinosaurs. The wagon ran off with the horses. I ran. I think if I'm the professor, I want to get a horse and return to other wagon the easy way...the way we came in at the arrow tree.

FRENCHY
What do you think we do?

COOKIE
I say we all eat now. We make small fire, eat meat, and get stronger. Two strongest men are Frenchy and Jose. You two run quickly to the wagon. Your direction will be at two o'clock, I think.

JOSE LAGANA
I believe that is right. I have tracked wild animals by using the sun and stars. I would say two also.

COOKIE
Good, now does anyone have matches?

FRENCHY
I do.

COOKIE
Make a fire and cut sticks to roast the meat. We
will eat fast. You and Jose will leave first.

FRENCHY
You and Ben will be alright? oui?

COOKIE
If you make it before the professor gets to the other
wagon, good. You can warn them. If professor makes it
before you, I pray you make good decision. If professor
asks about Cookie and Ben, we died in jungle.

BIG BEN
Save a piece of that lying dirt bag
for Big Ben to hit wit these guns.

He lifts up his huge fists. They cook the meat and eat it. Jose and
Frenchy say their good byes.

FRENCHY
Wish us luck.

Everyone hugs.

COOKIE
Now go. May my ancestors guide you.

BIG BEN
I be prayin' too.

They push back branches and blaze through the jungle to the wagon.

EXT GLEN TO THE RIGHT OF THE JUNGLE-MCROY'S
COMPANY-DAY

Everette, and Tex get in the stream with Juan.

                    EVERETTE KIRBY
            Let me see that. Oh yep, look at that
                beautiful grain and it's heavy!

                     TEX LAWSON
              Here, let me give a look see.

He inspects the golden infused rock and rotates it closely.

                     TEX LAWSON
                (cont)Pretty nice, huh?

He hands it back to a reaching Juan as he kicks up another, even
larger stone and holds it up.

                     TEX LAWSON
         (cont)Forget a gold pan, give me a damned gunny
          sack for these golden potatoes. WE'RE RICH!!!

                      EVERYONE
            Yahoo! Wow! look! Move over I want to get
                some too. Hey that's my spot!!

                    JUAN BARTELLI
                   I found it first!

BLAM! BLAM! BLAM! John McRoy shoots his pistol in the air.

JOHN MACROY
Now listen up. We've got to get
back to the arrow tree, meet the others and get back to
our world. I don't know what creatures lurk in the night
here, and I don't wish to find out...I only know that....

VIRGINIA DEVEN
Look....in the distance near the arrow tree.

There a man on horseback was galloping toward them.

TIMOTHY MACROY
It looks like... it is...it's the professor! But where are the others?

VIRGINIA DEVEN
This doesn't sound good.

All the others except John, Virginia and Tim are in the stream searching for gold. John walks over to the stream.

JOHN MACROY
For the love of Mike, would you three get
your take of these rocks and let's go.

EVERETTE KIRBY
Do we have gunney sacks or buckets in the wagon?

TIMOTHY MACROY
We do...I saw some near...

JOHN MACROY
Boy, go help Virginia get ready. We're leaving.

TIMOTHY MACROY
Yes Dad.

JOHN MACROY
Everette!

EVERETTE KIRBY
Yes sir?

JOHN MACROY
If you know what's good for you, leave that damned gold and
let's get out of here. We need to meet up with the others.

EVERETTE KIRBY
Boss, just let me take one bucket full?

The professor gallups up to everyone.

PROFESSOR PERKINS
Oh thank heavens you're here. We had terrible luck.
We were attacked by giant snakes 50 foot long! Then
after that by Tyrannasaurus Rex, two of them.

Virginia interrogates with a squinted eye.

VIRGINIA DEVEN
So where are the others?

PROFESSOR PERKINS
I'm afraid to tell you their fates. I went to get firewood
and barely got to the trees when two giant snakes
attacked the wagon killing Ben and Cookie.

TIMOTHY MACROY
NOT BEN AND COOKIE!

PROFESSOR PERKINS
Yes, and the giant snakes scattered the horses. Frenchy
and Jose made it out alive and headed for me in the
trees, but, they were attacked and eaten by two "T"
Rex dinosaurs. Nothing left to even bury.

TIMOTHY MACROY
OH NO!!! Ben, Frenchy, Jose and Cookie!

Tim starts to cry. Virginia embraces him and smells a rat.

JOHN MACROY
Professor spare the details you've upset the boy
and this is even hard for all of us to bear...but...
the guns? Didn't anyone get to the big guns?

PROFESSOR PERKINS
If you had seen the havoc, tearing
the wagon apart and killing the horses and then us.
Terrible I tell you! A haunting to a man's soul.

Juan, Tex and Everette didn't even look up enough to realize that
the professor had returned. They were furiously gathering GOLD.
Finally Everette looks up.

EVERETTE KIRBY
Look... It's the professor.

The others continue to fill their buckets.

TEX LAWSON
Howdy! Now don't bother me.

JUAN BARTELLI
We find lots of gold! See!

He holds up a giant nugget.

TEX LAWSON
Juan, do you know what
"Shut-up your fool mouth" means?

EVERETTE KIRBY
So where's Frenchy, Ben, Jose and Cookie?

PROFESSOR PERKINS
As I told John, they were
killed by prehistoric beasts.
I barely made it out with the last horse.
Um...Did you say you found gold?

EVERETTE KIRBY
Juan actually found it.
There's a small fortune in this stream.

PROFESSOR PERKINS
Really!?! Are there any more buckets left?

EVERETTE KIRBY
In the wagon.

The professor heads for the wagon. Young Tim comes to his Dad to
get permission to relieve himself in the trees about fifty yards away.

VIRGINIA DEVEN
Take your sixshooters
in case of a varmint.

TIMOTHY MACROY
I got 'em.

He pats them and reveals the bullet studded belt and holstered six shooters. He runs for the trees.

VIRGINIA DEVEN
John, the professor's lying. I don't believe his
story. He's leaving out too much.

JOHN MACROY
Aye! If the pot stinks, the soup is rotten! In this
case we may never know what happened to
Frenchy, Ben, Jose, and Cookie. Someone else should
have got to the guns. it just doesn't add up?

VIRGINIA DEVEN
I think we need to keep our eyes on him.
By the way, where are the Indians?

JOHN MACROY
Blasted! The savages left us.
Where did they go?

The professor emerges from around the wagon holding a pistol and bucket.

PROFESSOR PERKINS
Ok, John and Virginia I'll
take your six shooters and those rifles.

They reluctantly hand them over.

PROFESSOR PERKINS
(cont)...and don't forget that little derringer in
your right boot legging Miss Deven.

VIRGINIA DEVEN
Pray tell how you knew about that?

                    PROFESSOR PERKINS
                Oh...a little birdie who didn't know
                    I was picking his brain.

She slaps the tiny pistol in his hand.

                    VIRGINIA DEVEN
                        Here!

He points to the rifles on the saddled horses.

                    PROFESSOR PERKINS
                        Rifles too.

They take their rifles from the horses and give them up.

                    VIRGINIA DEVEN
                (under her breath) John, go along with
                    me on this. I'll always love you.

                    JOHN MACROY
                        Sure, but...

                    VIRGINIA DEVEN
                (Under her breath) Shh!! Trust me.

                    PROFESSOR PERKINS
                Now Virginia, take all the weapons and
                    empty the bullets out of them.
                            (MORE)

                PROFESSOR PERKINS (cont'd)
        Put it all in this gunny sack. Loose bullets, guns and rifles.

She does what he tells her to do.

VIRGINIA DEVEN
John, I hate you for getting me into this. I'm going to
get killed and for what?....A trip to dinosaur hell!

JOHN MACROY
Please love, don't be cross...I just..

VIRGINIA DEVEN
Keep away John, I don't care to be with you!

PROFESSOR PERKINS
Now Virginia, it's not all bad.
I've got a great team you can join.

Virginia And the Professor are talking as they walk over toward the
stream. Tex, Juan and Everette are gathering baseball-size rocks of gold.

PROFESSOR PERKINS
(cont) Hi Tex, Everette and
....what's your name?)

JUAN BARTELLI
Juan.

PROFESSOR PERKINS
Oh yes, Juan, now everyone
bring your buckets to me.
And Virginia get the gunny sacks ready.

He points the pistol at everyone.

PROFESSOR PERKINS
(cont) Take off your holsters, six shooters and any other
contraband and give it to Virginia over there. Virginia,
empty the guns and put everything into the sack.

With a smile on her face.

VIRGINIA DEVEN
You got it!

EVERETTE KIRBY
Never thought I'd see the day that
John's wife-to-be would be kissin' up to the likes of
a traitor. Your a professor of what? Hooligans?

PROFESSOR PERKINS
Come now Everette, what a mean spirited thing to say.

VIRGINIA DEVEN
Just give me your guns, Everette.

PROFESSOR PERKINS
Actually Everette, I'm more of an
entreprenuer than a professor.
Isn't that right, Tex? I like the sound of gold
better than dinosaur eggs don't you?!

TEX LAWSON
As long as we're makin money, like I told you before
Professor, that's why I came on this trip.

PROFESSOR PERKINS
Good! Our new plan is everyone
is going in the stream gathering gold. Tex, you're going to
turn the wagon around and bring it closer to the stream
so we can load up our "mother lode". Ha, Ha.

TEX LAWSON
I like the free help idea.

PROFESSOR PERKINS
So go do it Tex.

TEX LAWSON
Yee Haw! Get along dawgies!

EVERETTE KIRBY
So you're in on it too
Tex...I should have known.

TEX LAWSON
I came to be rich one way or
a-nother. I guess this is a-nother.

The Professor lifts his pistol toward Everette.

PROFESSOR PERKINS
Everette, how about shutting up that cow hole for a
mouth of yours. You and Juan gather up some more gold
before nightfall sets in. NOW DO IT! Bam!Bam!

He shoots two rounds into the air. They dump their buckets of
golden chunks in front of Virginia and the Professor and go back in
the stream for more.

EXT NEAR JUNGLE AND WAGON- DAY

Tex takes John to look for Tim driving the wagon.

JOHN MACROY
Son! Where are you?!

He comes out from behind a tree.

TIMOTHY MACROY
Here Dad.

TIMOTHY MACROY (VO)
I was wondering where everyone went. I could see some
in the distance by the stream. If I wasn't so deep in the
woods, I might have seen the professor show his true
colors. I saw Dad and Tex coming from the distance.

JOHN MAC ROY
Tim! Son are you out there? Tim!

TIMOTHY MAC ROY(VO)
That's better I thought. They're coming to get me. Things
change rapidly in the Cretacious Period I guess?

TEX LAWSON
Hey there, boy! Better git in the wagon.
We're joinin' the others younder.

He points to the group by the stream.John gets down from the wagon
to get close.

JOHN MACROY
Better get your things together Son...I...

TEX LAWSON
Say boy...Hand me up that
holster and six shooters.

TIMOTHY MACROY
NO!

He turns to his father.

TIMOTHY MACROY
(cont)
Dad, do I have to?

JOHN MACROY
(under his breath)
Run for the trees as soon as I take one of your guns.
(Full voice) Now give me the pistols, boy, so I can…

TIMOTHY MACROY
NO! I'm not giving up my sixshooters!

He runs for the woods and Tex's eyes follow him. He turns around to view life at the end of a sixshooter that John is aiming at his face.

JOHN MACROY
I'm sorry it worked out this way, Tex. How about
throwing down your pistols and your rifle.

He throws them down one at a time and hesitates with the rifle for a split second.

JOHN MACROY
I wouldn't even think on it laddie. I've shot a buffalo between
the eyes with one of these pea shooters and brought him
down with the first shot. Oh it's not a pretty sight for the
receiving end. Believe me! THROW IT DOWN!

Tex throws down the rifle.

JOHN MACROY
Now you get down from the
wagon toward me. No tricks!

John doesn't take his eyes off Tex. He turns his head and yells for Tim.

JOHN MACROY
Timmy! Come on back lad, I need for you…

In mid sentence Tim returns with Jose and Frenchy.

TIMOTHY MACROY
Look who I found!

JOHN MACROY
Great heavens above! God has answered our
prayers. Frenchy you're alive and Jose!

FRENCHY
What is going on John?

JOHN MACROY
The professor is no good Frenchy. And
Tex here is in cohoots with him.

FRENCHY
We know about the professor. He tried to kill us forcing us to
gather dinosaur eggs from a nest. Jose, Ben and I tried to escape
when he was distracted. Ben was shot in the back of the leg.

TIMOTHY MACROY
The professor said you all died and were eaten?

FRENCHY
Sacre bleu! He is such a liar. Cookie also escaped. He caught
up to us and we decided that Cookie would help wounded
Ben, while Jose and I raced ahead to warn every one.

JOHN MACROY
Believe me, we have time for the particulars later. Help me
tie this one up. Tex has to be hog tied with his own rope.

TEX LAWSON
You all aren't home free yet.

JOHN MACROY
And Frenchy let's gag him.

FRENCHY
Oui, Monsour MacRoy. It will be a pleasure.

JOSE LAGANA
And I'll get his legs.

5 MINUTES PASS

Tex is hog tied and in the back of the wagon.

JOHN MACROY
Jose, you and Tex are about the same size.
Take his cowboy hat and put it on.

The hat fits.

FRENCHY
Good. Now look tall and stupid.

Tex wiggles and screams into his gag wrap.

FRENCHY
(cont)
Oh it's not so bad Tex, you signed up with the wrong team. The
professor is an escaped convict killer. He confessed when he
robbed Ben and me that his name is Randall Starks. He killed
the real professor to escape from Colorado Penetentiary.

JOSE LAGANA
He tried to kill us. He would have killed you
too once he got what he wanted.

JOHN MACROY
Frenchy did you find any more guns in the wagon?

                        FRENCHY
         Oui, one dinosaur gun with two clips. We have Tex's two
           pistols and you have your son's two six shooters.

                      JOHN MACROY
             Now Frenchy I want you to stay here
           and set up camp to wait for Ben and Cookie. We
           will also return to this spot. Here's the plan.....

EXT GLEN TO THE RIGHT OF THE JUNGLE-STREAM
AREA- DAY

The wagon rolls up without incident, the Professor thinks Tex is
driving with John riding shotgun without a gun. The wagon stops
by the stream.

                     VIRGINIA DEVEN
           John, get Tim and start looking for gold
               in the stream before it gets dark.

                    PROFESSOR PERKINS
               And Tex, come down and
             lets load up what we got so far.

Jose swings his rifle on the Professor. John jumps down and also aims
his pistol at him.

                      JOHN MACROY
         Would you like to part with that pistol that you've
             been waving at everyone, Mr. Starks?

                     VIRGINIA DEVEN
               Who are you talking to?

JOSE LAGANA
The professor is not a professor. He's an escaped convict that
killed the real Professor Perkins and stole his identity.

PROFESSOR PERKINS
What a big cock and bull story. How do you suppose
I worked at the university studying dinosaurs? Why,
even Tim was in my college preparatory classes!

EVERETTE KIRBY
Hey you know what, we're getting out of this cold water.
Virginia, would you please give us our guns back?

VIRGINIA DEVEN
Not yet. The professor makes sense, and I don't know
what John and is up too, but I believe the professor.

John feels Virginia's great acting ability.

JOHN MACROY
Ok Missy, you've played the part we're good now. Let's get on
with it and get out of this place. I think the savages were smart
enough to leave while the gettin' was good. Now it's our turn.

VIRGINIA DEVEN
No, John, I'm not acting. The professor has much
more to offer me in life, than to be the big game
hunter's wife in a subservient existence.

She aims her gun at John and Jose. Tim comes out of the wagon and
tries to talk to her.

TIMOTHY MACROY
Virginia, what are you doing. My Dad loves
you and you love him, I thought.

JOHN MACROY
Son, get back in the wagon.

TIMOTHY MACROY
No Dad. I want Virginia for a mom.

She lets her gun down in a repentant motion.

VIRGINIA DEVEN
Oh Timmy, what was I thinking.

Before anyone knew what transpired the Professor shoots Virginia. BAM! He turns and shoots Jose and John. BAM! BAM! BAM. Jose is dead. John and Virginia are wounded.

TIMOTHY MAC ROY(VO)
It happened so fast. I just started running for
the jungle, crying between breaths.

PROFESSOR PERKINS
Tim you get back here! Come back!

He turns to Everette.

PROFESSOR PERKINS
Everette, no monkey business, go get the
boy and bring him back...on foot.

EVERETTE KIRBY
OK.

TIMOTHY MACROY (VO)
You know, I really didnt' understand what made me just get
up and start running. I never gave thought to my Dad and

Virginia who lay wounded. Jose was dead! I just snapped.
For whatever reason it's a good thing that I did.

EXT GLEN TO THE RIGHT OF THE JUNGLE-STREAM
AREA- DUSK

The professor barks orders.

PROFESSOR PERKINS
Juan, load up that damned
gold and Tex. Where is Tex?

Tex starts hammering his heels in the wagon to let him know where he is.

JUAN BARTELLI
Shouldn't I take care of John and Virginia first. They
are bleeding badly? I must bury my friend Jose!!

Tex starts banging on the wagon floor. Bang! Bang! Bang! The professor looks in the wagon to see Tex tied up.

PROFESSOR PERKINS
Hell's bells! Juan you take care of John and the girl. I'll deal
with Tex. Get the wounded and make a fire while you're
at it. I'm getting hungry and it soon to be nightfall.

JUAN BARTELLI
I must bury my friend Juan.

PROFESSOR PERKINS
After you get the fire and wounded set up.

JUAN BARTELLI
Yes,I will do that.

PROFESSOR PERKINS
Don't get pissy with me; just do what I
say comprende? (understand?)

JUAN BARTELLI
I understand.

PROFESSOR PERKINS
Good! NOW DO IT!

The professor unties Tex and removes his gag.

TEX LAWSON
It's damned dry with that gag.
Got some water over there?

The professor turns around to see a bucket of water with a drinking
ladle and cup. He pours him a cup.

PROFESSOR PERKINS
Drink this I've got to check on the others. Take one of
these guns, get Juan to help you load the gold.

That wagon's not leaving here empty!

TEX LAWSON
How about we get something to eat before we go back for gold?

PROFESSOR PERKINS
Fine, but let's use all the help we got before we
shoot them and make our getaway.

John and Juan hear the words and know their time is short. The professor and Tex leave the wagon with guns drawn. The night has fallen.
Sounds are ominous. OO-waa! OO--wa!!GRRRRR! Yipe, Yipe, Yipe!

TEX LAWSON
That's a nasty souding critter!

Strange new sounds pervade the darkness. Screams of unimaginable beasts, followed by the roar of the "T" Rex. lots of chirping and deep grunts add to the cacocphany of strangeness.

TEX LAWSON
What's out there?

PROFESSOR PERKINS
We don't have time to worry about that.

Juan puts Virginia down by the fire. She winces in pain with every movement.

JUAN BARTELLI
Here Miss Deven, this should be good for you for the time being. Let me put this wrap around your wound. It will help to stop some of this bleeding. I found some leaves that look like aloe vera. It may help you.

VIRGINIA DEVEN
Thank you Juan... Where is my Johnny?
John are you there?

Virginia hallucinates and falls asleep. Juan hurries to get John. He tries to lift the big Scotsman to no avail.

JUAN BARTELLI
Can someone help me to put him by the fire? He is too heavy for me alone.

PROFESSOR PERKINS
Tex get him over there would you?

TEX LAWSON
I guess.

He walks over to the wagon and the two of them carry John and place him next to Virginia. He sees her and feels so helpless.

JOHN MACROY
Oh Lassie, if you hadn't have acted the part
and get carried away. I'll still marry ya'

He softly strokes her face with his good arm. She wakes and is barely conscious.

VIRGINIA DEVEN
John, can you ever forgive me?
I want you and Tim...

JOHN MACROY
Save you strength my love.
I will always love you.

VIRGINIA DEVEN
Thank God.

She passes out.

PROFESSOR PERKINS
Juan you and Tex....

Lightning strikes across the sky and heavy winds whip through the glen. Winds gust upward to 40 to 60 miles per hour. Juan moves quickly to the wounded.

JUAN BARTELLI
They must go in the wagon professor.

PROFESSOR PERKINS
Make sure there's plenty of space for tomorrow's
gold, or just leave them outside.

JUAN BARTELLI
Hurry , Help me!

Tex runs over and they first take John. They carry him up into the covered wagon with the professor helping from the inside of the wagon. It is slow going with the rain and John's heavy anatomy.

JUAN BARTELLI
We've got to get Virginia.
It's bad out there!

They set him down and go back for Virginia. They have a lanturn and hold it up toward her in time to see a strange man that has strapped Virginia to a stick sled. This Robinson Crusoe type runs away with her into the darkness?

TEX LAWSON
Did you see that?!!!

JUAN BARTELLI
Si! He looked like a jungle man.

PROFESSOR PERKINS
Robinson Crusoe perhaps.

TEX LAWSON
What in the Sam hell are we doin' now boss?

PROFESSOR PERKINS
Head for the trees where Everette and the kid are.

The horses are spooked by the lightning and are slowing down the effort.

EXT JUNGLE STRIP OF TREES-NIGHT

Everette calls for Tim. He searches and calls in the night.

EVERETTE KIRBY
Tim! Tim! Are you out there?! Tim! Tim!

Cookie and Ben come out of the bushes and Tim is with them.

BIG BEN
I sure do like seeing your
happy face once more.

COOKIE
Me too!

TIMOTHY MACROY
And me!

EVERETTE KIRBY
It's great to see you three also. The weather is
so bad. We need to make a shelter.

FRENCHY
I've got my Bowie knife. I'll cut the main saplings.
Someone else find the large leaves.

BIG BEN
I've got da leaves.

Ben hobbles off on his crutch to get them.

COOKIE
Make a large shelter. I still have some lizard meat
I can cook up in a rain free lean to.

FRENCHY
It's coming up Monseur Wu. I must make it
large enough for five or six people.

He walks back under the shelter of three large pre-historic fern trees. The wind is squalling and the trees bend and sway. Lightning flares up in the night sky for a temporary view of the scenery. The thunder spooks the dinosaurs in the distance as they complain after every clap.

TIMOTHY MACROY
Can I help?

FRENCHY
Oui. You can gather branches
large enough to put these large
fern leaves on. I will notch them to fit. Hurry!

COOKIE
I will help get them.

BIG BEN
We's got to save some dry leaves to start the fire. Well
catch a death of cold if we don't get a fire soon.

EVERETTE KIRBY
Just keep them branches and
leaves a comin'. We'll get 'em up

The work goes well and the shelter takes great shape under the protection of the trees. Some dry tinder and branches were found. Frenchy tries to start it.

FRENCHY
Sacre Bleu! (holy blue) my matches are wet.

COOKIE
How about these?

He pulls a closed metal cannister from his pocket. It contains dry matches and a striker stone.

FRENCHY
If you were a woman I would kiss you. Mmmm wa!

He throws him a kiss. They start the fire in the hollow of the tree they lean against. The fire smokes until the branches burn hot. They all fit inside. All enjoy the warmth and cover from the elements.

TIMOTHY MACROY
I'm worried about Dad and Virginia.
What if they bleed to death!

BIG BEN
Yo' daddy is a smart man young Tim. He will find a way.

FRENCHY
I would count on it.

COOKIE
Me, too!

EVERETTE KIRBY
John was talking last I saw him. He was worried about you
Tim. You have to be strong. Fellas we better think of a plan.
I came here to fetch Tim and they ain't stayin out in that bad
weather too very long. They'll be headed to these trees.

I'm goin' out for a look-see.

BIG BEN
You be careful yoo hear now.

He climbs out into the rugged storm, rushing from tree to tree.
He's well concealed. He looks back and can see the fire through the
make shift shelter with white wisps of smoke being blown sideways
above the shelter. The neighs from the wagon horses could be heard.
Everette takes a closer look.He sees the Professor and wagon.

PROFESSOR PERKINS
Tex, tie the wagon horses to one of those trees.
Juan try and quiet the animals down. Bring them
in the shelter of the trees if you can.

TEX LAWSON
Look over there. Looks like a fire.

PROFESSOR PERKINS
Go get Everette and the boy. Take your Colt with you.

JOHN MACROY
You take good care of me boy. Hear me now.

TEX LAWSON
He's gonna' be just fine.

Tex leaves toward the light not knowing Everette follows him.

PROFESSOR PERKINS
No problem, John. If Tex doesn't come back, I'll
shoot you. No more worries about anything.

JOHN MACROY
You're rottn to the core, Mr. Starks.

PROFESSOR PERKINS
Aw, just call me the professor for old time sakes.

EXT JUNGLE STRIP OF TREES-NIGHT

Tex approaches the shelter. They are unaware of his advance.

TIMOTHY MACROY
Frenchy, do you think Virginia is going to make it?

FRENCHY
I can't say. I have not seen her since our return.

Tex lifts up part of the shelter at gunpoint.

TEX LAWSON
Welcome, Ben, Cookie, Tim,
Frenchy and ..? Where's Everette.

Conk! Tex falls to the ground unconscious.

EVERETTE KIRBY
Right here Tex. Quick get him in.
Frenchy come with me.

They leave the shelter and talk behind the shelter of a tree.

FRENCHY
What do you think my friend.

EVERETTE KIRBY
We have got to get the wagon back and rescue John. The
Professor is crazy. He will shoot anyone for any reason.
I don't see that we are safe around him. Look
what happened to Jose, John and Virginia.

FRENCHY
Right. I think we should lure him out of the
wagon and nab him. He still has John.

The professor suddenly appears from behind a tree with pistol drawn.

PROFESSOR
Life sure is full of surprises. We need to prepare for the
unexpected don't we. Now Frenchy, hand over the knife handle
first and Everette I'll take that six shooter in you belt.

Frenchy and Everette look up above the Professor and see a tree climbing dino descending. It's ready to pouce on him. Frenchy hands him his knife just as the aligator type dinosaur attacks. Frenchy retracts it to his sheath.

PROFESSOR
Ahhh! Ahhh! Help! Get him off!

EVERETTE KIRBY
You're right, Life sure is full of surprises.

The climbing lizard is mauling his face and left arm. The professor manages to free up his right arm and shoots the beast three times at point blank. BLAM! BLAM! BLAM! The giant lizard drops to the ground missing everyone. The professor's face is bleeding profusely, running down and spattered by the pelting rain.

PROFESSOR
Surprise! Blam! Blam!

He shoots Everette in the neck. and turns to shoot Frenchy. Frenchy jumps for the brush and rangles through it in a low crawl position. The Professor sees where Frenchy stops.

PROFESSOR
(cont)
You're not getting away that easily, Frenchy!

His hiding place revealed by lightning flashing in the night. He takes aim. BAM! BAM! BAM! The Professor stands upright over Frenchy then slumps to his knees and falls over.

BIG BEN
Thank you young Tim for the use of your six shooter.
I know the good book say to love you enemies, but I
hate 'da man. He's no professor, he's 'da devil.

Frenchy gets up and sees Everette dead.

FRENCHY
I guess it was not my time to go.
I am sorry for Everette, my friend.

The professor turns slightly and shoots Frenchy dead.

BIG BEN
LOOK OUT! BAM!

Ben goes over to the professor and shoots him dead. BAM! BAM! BAM! He then sobs and weeps. Cookie comes out and consoles the living.

BIG BEN
Lord, why did dey hafta die? Oh dear, God, it's a hard
day to be alive. I'm missin' my friends and brothers.

Tim cries along with Ben. Cookie takes charge and thinks this through. It was still raining but the worst of the storm has passed.

COOKIE
We must find the others. The wagon is close
by. Let's find them and leave this place.

BIG BEN
I'm wit' you on 'dat. Let's get Tex and head for the
wagon. I gotta first put some leaves and brush over
these dead bodies and say a prayer or somethin'.

30 minutes later

The bodies are covered and Ben takes his hat off and bows his head.
Cookie does the same. Tim just stares and listens. He's in shock.

COOKIE
You pray Ben. I'll listen very good.

BIG BEN
Dear Lord, we ask that you accept my brothers,
Frenchy and Everette, into your Heavenly Gates. They
be rowdy sometimes but have good hearts, helpin'
people and all that, risking their very souls.
Overlook the poker games and hard drinkin' at times.
We is not as perfect as you. Forgive us our sins and
forgive me for I still hates the professor. Amen

TIMOTHY MACROY (VO)
I saw everything. Heck, I was just a kid. My Dad and Virginia
and Ben are shot. Everette, Frenchy and Jose are dead. My teacher
from Belmont Prepatory school is dead and so is his imposter. My
head was swimming. I was in shock. Then it was utter confusion.
You know when you're numb it is hard to have genuine feelings,
let alone make decisions. The nightmare just wouldn't stop.

COOKIE
Ben, get Tex from the shelter, then we'll go to the wagon.

Ben walks over to the shelter and sees a large forty foot snake with Tex in his mouth. He couldn't cry out, being gagged; the thunder was so noisy, no one could hear him.

BIG BEN
Let's get outta here. Tex is in the snake"s
belly. We want to leave now.

Big Ben, Cookie, and Tim head out. A "T" Rex smells the bodies and emerges from the jungle with RROOAAR! and sniffs at the burial sites and proceeds to dig it up with his large legs. Meanwhile the large snake feels threatened, vomits up Tex, and attacks the "T"Rex.

BIG BEN
Come mista Tim. Let's get outa' here!

The Cowboy troop passes by and sees the battle of a large opponent wrapped in the snakes coils fighting for its' life. They leave the trees and see the wagon.

COOKIE
Look the wagon!

They run for it. Ben hobbles quickly with his crutch and Cookie and Tim are along side of him. Tuffy starts to bark as soon as he hears them comming, Juan looks out.

JUAN BARTELLI
Mr. MacRoy they're coming.

John has just woke up from a deep sleep.

JOHN MACROY
Who's coming?

JUAN BARTELLI
Your son, Big Ben and Cookie.

JOHN MACROY
Where's Virginia?... And Everette?
and the Professor and Tex?

JUAN BARTELLI
I do not know.

Ben, Cookie and Tim, arrive at the wagon. Tim goes races to hug his father. They embrace.

TIMOTHY MACROY
Dad You're alive,I thought
I'd never see you again.

BIG BEN
How are you doin', sir?

JOHN MACROY
A wee bit sore but I'll live.

COOKIE
Good to see you Mr. MacRoy.

JOHN MACROY
And good to see you Cookie.

Tim looks around.

TIMOTHY MACROY
Where's Virginia?

JOHN MACROY
Where is Virginia?

JUAN BARTELLI
Senor MacRoy, you were lying side by side with
Virginia near the stream. The storm came up and
Tex and I carried you into the wagon. We went back for
her and saw a jungle man pulling her away on a Indian
sled. The Professor called him robin's son cruso?

John wakes up with the shocking news.

JOHN MACROY
Another human in this place, that's absurd. What
jungle man? Where? I can't go without her!
For heaven's sake man, where is she?

JUAN BARTELLI
John, she was laying next to you and...

The dog starts barking wildly. Cookie starts to pull the rear wagon
curtain open ever so slowly, He sees a giant face of a "T" Rex sniffing
the back of the wagon. It acts as if it can't see them. Tuffy won't stop
barking. John talks softly to Ben.

JOHN MACROY
Ben, do you see that dinosaur rifle over there?
It's ready to go... take it off safety,
release the slide and shoot.

Ben slowly reaches for the gun. He picks it up and releases the safety
and slide. This agitates the "T" Rex which starts to roar. ROARRRRR!
Ben opens fire. BAM! BAM! BAM! BAM!
Young Tim also shoots his six shooter.

TIMOTHY MAC ROY
I'm shootin' too!

POP! POP! POP! POP! The horses get startled and take off pulling the wagon wildly. Cookie holds a lantern out the back of the wagon to see a dead "T" Rex with another nosing around the fresh kill. It looks up at Cookies lantern and pursues.

COOKIE
Get ready one more time!
Another lizard comes quickly for us.

Ben is now trying to guide the team of horses. Juan goes up with him.

JUAN BARTELLI
Ben, go back and shoot the monster. I'll take over.

He gets the gun and returns. He checks the ammo and pokes the barrel out the back of the wagon. Some moonlight shows through the broken clouds. It reflects on the pursuing dinosaur.

BIG BEN
I see him now. Come and get it.

JOHN MACROY
Wait until he's about twenty feet from the wagon and aim for the head. Steady! Steady! OK! Let him have it!

BAM!BAM!BAM!BAM!BAM!BAM! They look with the lanturn at a crumpled pile of flesh. Now something's bumping the wagon from all sides and the horses are stressed. THEY'RE IN A STAMPEDE OF DINOSAURS. DUCK BILLED, TRICERATOPS, PARASAURUS AND MANY MORE CROWD DANGEROUSLY AROUND THE WAGON. Juan calls back.

JUAN BARTELLI
What do I do?

JOHN MACROY
Don't scare the horses any more than they
already are. We'll have to ride it out.

BIG BEN
I'm comin'. Those horses know me.
They hear my voice and listen.

He takes the reins

BIG BEN
(cont.)Ok children, It's Big Ben.
Yah! Yah! We gonna' be jus' fine.

The stampede turns the direction of the arrow tree. The herd opens up
and splits behind them. It's two "T" Rexes and they're chasing the wagon.

TIMOTHY MACROY
Ben come back quick. More dinos' to shoot.

BIG BEN
Juan take the reins again, I be commin' back in a hurry!

Juan and Ben switch while Cookie gets the gun for Ben.

COOKIE
It's the last clip of ammo we have. Make it count.

BIG BEN
I will Mr. Wu.

JOHN MACROY
Wait 'till the creature is almost upon us. Shoot for the eyes.

BIG BEN
I hears ya' Mr MacRoy.

He cocks the rifle, releasing the slide.

JOHN MACROY
Steady, steady... OK, let him have it.

The "T" Rex roars as his flesh pops, ROARRR! BAM!BAM!BAM!

CRASH!!!tinkle BIM BAM! NEIGH! NEIGH! gallop, gallop, gallop.

TIMOTHY MACROY (VO)
We didn't see it coming. It was dark. Now utter
confusion. I was ready to give up. I thought am I dead
already? I forgot who I was and where I was.

JUAN BARTELLI
What is that?! Sancti Maria! (Holy mother of God!)

CRASH! SMASH! NEIGH! SCREAM! AHHHHHHHH! The
horses continue to scream unto their death.

The horses were badly wounded when they hit the rock. The wagon
was in bad shape but Still had some cover.

JOHN MACROY
Oh Lord! What Happened? What a mess!

COOKIE
I light this lantern.

He holds it out to illuminate the crash scene.

JOHN MACROY
Tim, are you alright?

TIMOTHY MACROY
Just fine Dad.

JOHN MACROY
Ben, how did you do in the crash?

BIG BEN
I think I cracked my ribs, but I'm gonna be jus' fine , Sir.

JOHN MACROY
Cookie, are you OK?

COOKIE
Yes but, ow! I think I broke my wrist on my left arm.
I' be good. Cookie heals fast cause he's a
Chinaman, Ha,Ha, Ha. Ow!

BIG BEN
You are a funny one, too.

John hobbles to the front and calls to Juan.

JOHN MACROY
Juan, Juan are you ok out there?

No response. You could hear horses moaning that weren't quite dead yet.

Ben takes the lanturn and looks up front. He finds Juan thrown against the large rocks of the crash. Ben removes his hat for respect as he returns to the wagon.

BIG BEN
You can stop callin' for Juan...
He left this earth to see his maker.

John pulls out a pocket watch.

JOHN MACROY
It's 5:00 am and we have an hour before sunrise. Tim
you and Cookie are healthy enough to walk to the arrow
tree. Walk there and wait for us or the indians.

TIMOTHY MACROY
Without Cookie you have no legs. How can you cook
or build? Besides you can't be near the dead horses for
too long. The "T" Rex will come and your not able to
fight them off very well with limited fire power.

JOHN MACROY
We have one pistol I believe.

BIG BEN
Mr. MacRoy, look what I just found! It's a
gunny sack full of weapons and bullets!

He holds them up. It's the firearms Viginia had collected.

JOHN MACROY
GREAT! That's the best news so far. When
it's daylight we'll go through it.

COOKIE
Maybe we should get ammo clips and find big guns now,
in case we get visit from big dinosaurs. Here is the light.

BIG BEN
I'll help.

JOHN MACROY
That's fine.

ONE HOUR LATER- 6:00 am

JOHN MACROY
Son when you and "TUFFY" head for the "Arrow"
tree, Don't let the Dinosaurs gang up on you. Stay
to the outside of the trees to avoid an ambush.

TIMOTHY MACROY
Yes, father.

JOHN MACROY
Wait for us 'til around noon. Hopefully the Savages will
be there before us. Now Go before I don't let you.

John tears up.

JOHN MACROY
(cont')God speed! Now be off boy.
I love you Timothy MacRoy!

They hug and he turns to go with Cookie and Ben also hugging Him.

COOKIE
Here is some Chinese Candy. It will give you
energy. Has gensing and green tea.

Thanks
TIMOTHY MACROY

BIG BEN
Take this canteen of water. You don't know how
long before yo' gonna' need some moisture.

TIMOTHY MACROY
Thank you, Ben!

JOHN MACROY
Now go son, before the rest of the creatures wake up.

TIMOTHY MACROY
Don't worry Dad, I will do this.

He and "Tuffy" leave.

EXT JUNGLE STRIP OF TREES-DAWN

Tim starts his walk. It's about ten miles to the "arrow tree". He walks to the outside of the trees and heads due north. He can hear the small bat-like flying lizards getting situated in the trees.

TIMOTHY MAC ROY
Tuffy, come...we 've got to get to that arrow tree.

The loud flock of flying lizards pays no attention to the boy and his dog. Suddenly the whole swarm of perched flying lizards exits the tree and swirls into the air. BAM!(pause) BAM!(pause) BAM!(pause)BAM!

TIMOTHY MAC ROY
I know what it is Tuffy... they're shootin' the horses.

No longer would the wounded steads suffer.

TIMOTHY MACROY(VO)
I could remember walking and praying for Juan,
Frenchy ,and Everette. I asked God to have mercy
on them and all persons banged up but still alive.
Virginia, Ben, Cookie and Dad all needed a break.

TIMOTHY MACROY
We finally made it to the arrow tree "Tuffy". Look... no
one is here. I wonder where the Indians went to?

The dog starts barking and chases two small dinosaurs away from the tree and into the jungle.
TIMOTHY MACROY

(cont.) Tuffy come back here.
Tuffy! Tuffy! You dumb dog!

The weather starts clouding up. A thunder storm moves in. Lightning,wind squalls and hail appear. Tim gets cover and sits down against the arrow tree. He calls to Tuffy with no response. He's still in shock and losing hope of finding his dog. He sleeps.

EXT CHURCH SETTING IN DREAM - DAY

He dreams of his father and Virginia. They are descending the steps of a cathedral and scores of people are cheering, throwing rice, applauding and congratulating. Tim saw himself with a smile from ear to ear. He was so happy his face hurt from smiling so much. His Dad came over to him.

JOHN MACROY
Son, say hello to your new Mom.

He eagerly hugs her as she says, "I love you, Timmy. Can I be your new Mom?"

TIMOTHY MACROY
YOU BET!

The whole wedding party celebrates.

TIMOTHY MACROY
This is grand!

Fireworks go off in the sky (in his dream)

EXT AT THE ARROW-TREE - DAY

BLUE WOLF
Washita. (White Boy) Washita (White boy)

Tim wakes from his deep sleep to see BLUE WOLF trying to wake him. He hears gunfire in the distance. The same sounds as the fireworks in his dream. Six mounted indian braves accompany BLUE WOLF. One brave, BLACK FEATHER dismounts and interprets as BLUE WOLF speaks.

BLACK FEATHER
I will speak for my brother BLUE WOLF.

BLUE WOLF
We went through the clouds back to our village.I got another horse and returned to help the Great White Hunter who saved my life. WHERE IS YOUR FATHER AND THE REST?

Black Feather interprets.

TIMOTHY MACROY
My Dad, two others and
I are the only survivors. Many deaths.

Black Feather Interprets.

BLUE WOLF
AYE ya ho ya!!!(Where are they now?)

BLACK FEATHER
He is sorry to hear this. Where are they now?

TIMOTHY MACROY
Our wagon crashed over there.

He points about ten miles away

TIMOTHY MACROY
(cont)I walked here to get help.

Multiple gun shots are heard.

BLUE WOLF
We must help. Ride hard, and fast!

Black Feather reaches to Tim and pulls him up on his horse. They proceed, yelping all the way. The Indians and young Tim gallop to the cowboy's rescue.

TIMOTHY MAC ROY
There they are!

They get about 50 yards from the crashed wagon and see gunfire from within the battered vessel. It's a pack of "Raptors" tearing apart the dead horses and trying to attack John, Ben and Cookie every now and then.

BLUE WOLF
(Dakota tongue)
Circle the wagon and shoot the lizard beasts.

Arrows flew and rifle shot met their mark. Those in the wagon cheered.

JOHN MACROY
That's my boy he got the
Indians, we're going home!

BIG BEN
He has mo' injuns this time too!

COOKIE
Now I open Chinese restaurant, marry
wife and make Chinese babies!

Outside the Indians shoot and the raptors are going down. Only two left. One raptor runs away the other looks at BLUE WOLF with fixed evil cat-like eyes.

TIMOTHY MAC ROY
BLUE WOLF, look out!!!

He pounces 25 feet into the air about to land on BLUE WOLF. Three arrows hit him and knock him down, but he manages one more leap. POW! POW! POW!POW!POW!POW! The raptor drops dead. They look to see who fired the last shots.

TIMOTHY MACROY
I would have fired more but I ran out.

EVERYONE
Hooray! Yes! Hooray! Let's go!

BLUE WOLF speaks in the Dakota language.

BLUE WOLF
You are a shadow of your father. Be strong as a twister
cloud and gentle as deer with her newborn.
Thank you young MacRoy for your protection.

He motions the other braves to come and listen.
Help the wounded, double up on our horses. We must go now. The giant lizards are restless.

TIMOTHY MACROY (VO)
We all climbed on the road to that magic passage that would
take us back to the hard life we once complained about. The
wounded limped along with a driving force...we're going home!

BIG BEN
We be there soon, no worries!

In a short ride they were at the "Arrow Tree". They looked for the passage way.

BIG BEN
Well I'll be...where did it go?

It was nowhere to be found. They dismounted and felt the air. No where in sight was the corridor to the 19th century. Panic was setting in on the faces of the expedition.

BIG BEN
Listen... I hears something
It sounds like a dog barkin'.

A faint bark is heard. Bark Bark! It sounds like a dog in a locked room barking to get out.

TIMOTHY MACROY
"Tuffy" Tuffy"

Tuffy comes flying into their world but he is 100 feet further down from where they are.

JOHN MACROY
The bloody dog is showin' the way. Let's
go before the opening changes.

Tuffy heads back through as easy as bringing in the morning newspaper. The dog pops back to see if they are coming. He wants his masters to follow.

Everyone's on horseback and they pursue the dog. RRROOAARRR!!!!!!!!!!! an unusually large "T" Rex charges the group from out of nowhere. He stands at least fifty feet, and ten feet taller than any they have encounted before!

BLUE WOLF
Circle him, and let the wounded
down so we can fight!

It's truly a king of "T"Rex dinosaurs. The Indians race in circles around
the huge predator, and release their arrows and bullets from horseback.

JOHN MAC ROY
They bloody better look out.Not too close!

RROOARR! The monstrous brute snaps at each rider. His face and
neck are filled with arrows. "T" Rex reaches in a split second. Snap,
chomp! AAAAAAAHH! The nameless Indian gives his life and his
horse narrowly escapes.

BIG BEN
Did you see dat? This bad boy scares me.

The brute chomps him down in three gulps while more arrows fill
him like a pin cushion.

BLUE WOLF
(in Dakota tongue)
Let the others and the boy go free.
they must escape while we fight the devil lizard.
Black Feather lead them to the dogs opening.

The braves that carried the MacRoy party led John, Cookie, Ben and
Tim to the outside the action.

JOHN MACROY
(shouting)
We've got to get through that bloody opening.

Bark! Bark! Bark! Tuffy comes through again. The "T" Rex bends down to snap at him. Tuffy runs between his legs and bites his toe. The monster kicks him off as more arrows meet their mark.

BIG BEN
Look that giant lizard is in front of 'da way out!

TIMOTHY MACROY
That does it!

TIMOTHY MACROY (VO)
Something inside me just snapped. I remembered
I had three bullets left in my holster belt.

He takes them out and loads one pistol. No one is watching him. Their eyes are on the gargantuan reptile blocking their way.

EXT - FLASHBACK -SHOOTING LESSON AT THE RIVER

VIRGINIA DEVEN
Now I want you to pretend you're drawing a dot on
the wafer with a pencil but the pencil is your rifle.
Pull the trigger when you want to draw. Ready?

She throws the wafer into the air. BANG! It's a hit.

TIMOTHY MACROY (VO)
That's it! He's vulnerable in the eyes!
THOSE ARE MY WAFERS!

Loaded with three bullets and pistol in hand he walks toward the huge beast. Now Dad and the rest see him.

JOHN MACROY
Son come back! Don't! Dear God above, save my
son! He doesn't stand a bloody chance!

Tuffy again bites the monster's toes. It kicks him off toward Tim. He rolls and low crawls to Tim. The prehistoric monstrosity follows the dog with his head low to the ground and arrows flying. Tim quick fires BAM! Into the right eye.

JOHN MAC ROY
(cont)
Make a run for it Son!!!

The monster stands up inexcruciating pain. It then lowers his head to chomp Tim. BAM! BAM! the last two bullets enter his left eye. The beast stands up and staggers like the town drunk, falters and collapses with a huge BOOM! The ground shakes.

EVERYONE
Horray! Yippee! Yip! YIP! Hiya! Hiya! Hiya!(Indian
victory chant) HIYa woona! Hiya!

Huge flocks of flying reptiles scream from the jungle heights and fly around squawking.

They all danced and hugged around the Goliath of "T" Rexes. THEY hug Tim and lift him up in a victory celebration .

EVERYONE
He's A HERO!

BIG BEN
Mr.Tim, You is like David who killed Golliath
with some stones. You saved our skins!

COOKIE
Tim, you bring good luck and fortune to all of us.
You are no longer boy. You can sit with the men.

John walks over with tears in his eyes.

JOHN MACROY
Come here son of mine.
I just love you to death. Ya' had me worried
(MORE)

JOHN MACROY (cont'd)
seein' you doin' damage to that
big galoot with just a pea shooter.

TIMOTHY MACROY
I love you too Dad.

ARF! ARF! BARK!BARK! Tuffy gets their attention.He wants to leave as he goes in and out of the passage through time.

John walks over to BLUE WOLF. Black Feather Interprets.

JOHN MACROY
BLUE WOLF we must leave now
before the creature's older brother looks for him and
then we've got another bloody one to fight.

BLUE WOLF smiles and grips john's Hands. Black Feather Interprets.

BLUE WOLF
You are a great man MacRoy,
and your son carries your greatness.

He releases his grip and speaks to his braves.

BLUE WOLF
(cont)Get on your horses, bring
McRoy's people and we must go.

They all pass through the time warp caravan style.

TIMOTHY MACROY (VO)
We all filed through that tear in time. Everyone that survived:
My Dad, Big Ben, Cookie and I went back to the modern
world of 1880. We kissed the ground; all cheated death.
The nightmare was over; never again would we return. The
Chief's son BLUE WOLF went home to Red Eagle to be
with his people. We did avoid a Dakota Sioux uprising.

EXT DAKOTA SIOUX CAMP -DAY

BLUE WOLF goes to his Father Red Eagle and hugs. They walk together.

TIMOTHY MACROY (VO)
Big Ben came to work on our ranch

EXT MACROY RANCH IN THE SOUTH DAKOTA PLAINS -DAY

Ben is mending fences and waves at John and Tim as they ride up on
horseback.

TIMOTHY MACROY (VO)
Cookie went to town to
find a site for his restaurant.

EXT WHISKEY FLATS TOWN -DAY

Cookie is talking to store owners and looking for his restaurant
location.

EXT MACROY RANCH IN THE SOUTH DAKOTA PLAINS -DAY

John, Tim and Ben are working a small herd of about 30 head of cattle.

TIMOTHY MACROY (VO)
Dad and I talked about him selling his gun shops and settling
down on the ranch. There was just something missing.

INT. WHISKEY CREEK BAR, WHISKEY CREEK SOUTH DAKOTA- DAY

John MacRoy sits at a table with Big Ben, Cookie and Tim.

JOHN MACROY
Well we made it out alive and here's the $750 dollars for each of you I promised upon return, Tim included. It was one hell of a ride.......and you all have memories you can never forget. I'm gettin as much rest as I can get....

BIG BEN
I'm in agreement to that

COOKIE
I like to do same.

JOHN MACROY
...Before I go back to find Virginia.

They each look at one another in a state of wonderment.

THE END